*"See, Martak? All of me wants
to see you die," said Claybore.*

"And you will—you will die as only an immortal can.
You will live forever and be in complete pain for all
eternity. Nothing will save you. You will cry in the
dark for surcease and never find it. You will die, not
in body but in mind. Die, Martak, die!"

Lan couldn't stop the surging attack, but he deflected
it enough to keep from succumbing. Knowing his
strength was nowhere near adequate to destroy Claybore as he'd thought, cunning took over. Lan Martak
turned aside the assault and redirected it to the hopping, kicking leg.

"No!" came the shriek as Claybore realized what was
happening.

His leg vanished in a sizzling cloud of greasy black
smoke, lost forever.

"Your skin is gone. I have your tongue. Now your
left leg is destroyed. Who is losing, Claybore?"

Ace Science Fiction Books by Robert E. Vardeman

Cenotaph Road Series

CENOTAPH ROAD
THE SORCERER'S SKULL
WORLD OF MAZES
IRON TONGUE
FIRE AND FOG
PILLAR OF NIGHT

PILLAR OF NIGHT
ROBERT E. VARDEMAN

ACE SCIENCE FICTION BOOKS
NEW YORK

PILLAR OF NIGHT

An Ace Science Fiction Book/published by arrangement with
the author

PRINTING HISTORY
Ace Original/November 1984

ISBN: 0-441-66397-4

Ace Science Fiction Books are published by The Berkley Publishing Group,
200 Madison Avenue, New York, N.Y. 10016.
PRINTED IN THE UNITED STATES OF AMERICA

For eight who have meant a great deal to me.

mks
a-n k, rw(v)
bak
kih, raj, cdb
kea

CHAPTER ONE

"Claybore has baited a trap and waits for you," Kiska k'Adesina told Lan Martak. "You will die if you try to recover the legs."

"How do you know?" Lan demanded. The young mage tried to shake his oddly tender feelings toward the woman and failed. Claybore had laid a geas on him too potent to fight, too subtle to work around. Kiska k'Adesina was his mortal enemy, the commander of Claybore's grey-clad soldiers, a vicious foe—and he felt protective toward her. And more.

Sweat beaded on his forehead as he realized how much he loved—was forced to love!—the woman who had repeatedly tried to kill him.

"It's all part of Claybore's master plan. He wants you incapacitated. If you rush in foolishly, without planning, without taking enough precautions, then you will be . . . no more."

"What do you care?" Lan raged, more at his own impotence in dealing with Kiska than at the woman. He fought down any thought of failure. The slightest pause, the most

1

minute of hesitations and he would lose this coming battle.

At the center of the conflict lay Claybore's legs. The other sorcerer had been dismembered and his parts strewn along the infinite length of the Cenotaph Road. Over the years, through the millennia, Claybore had slowly reunited his parts. Others had attempted to stop him; they had died. Only Lan Martak stood between Claybore and domination of not a single world but myriads of them. The battle had been long and difficult, with victories for both of them. Claybore had rejoined his arms to his torso; the Kinetic Sphere, allowing him to move between worlds at will, throbbed heartlike in his chest. Lan had destroyed the sorcerer's skin and in his own mouth Lan tasted the metallic tang of the magical tongue once used by Claybore to speak spells and world-wrecking curses.

Lan felt increasingly inadequate as a mage. The major victories were his opponent's. What did he really know of magics? He had been raised on a forest world and had learned only minor fire and healing spells. This arena of magical battle was alien to him still. And so much rested on his shoulders. He alone could prevent Claybore from regaining his legs. This last addition would make the dismembered sorcerer almost whole—and invincible.

"You can't face him. You're not good enough," Kiska kept saying over and over. She tugged at his sleeve and tried to hold him back. He jerked free. Lan Martak said nothing as he spun and started through the maze inside the hollowed mountain of Yerrary. The gnomes who made this their home had spent centuries chewing out corridors and had created a twisting domain that was as much a part of their heritage as the forests were his. Lan quickly forgot ordinary sight and depended more and more on a magical scrying spell to lead him through the turnings.

At first he walked with faltering steps, then became more confident and strode with his usual ground-devouring pace. Kiska struggled to keep up with him but said nothing.

"The chamber we seek is near," he said after they had traversed long corridors.

Kiska clung to him, barely noticed. Lan Martak moved on for the final confrontation. Claybore could not permit him to enter that chamber unopposed. To do so meant the disembodied sorcerer lost all.

"Through that arch," Lan Martak said, pointing. His hand glowed a dull purple in response to the war spell on the doorway. "Go through and die."

"You can take off the spell?" Kiska k'Adesina asked anxiously.

"It is a multilayered spell," he said, examining it carefully. "Very tricky. And very clever. One small slip and we die horribly."

Kiska tensed, her hands balled to strike out. Lan noticed and she relaxed and let her arms hang limply at her sides. He faced the doorway and began his chants.

Slowly at first, then with increasing assurance he peeled away the layers of the magics. Like onion skins, the spells fell away until only the bare stone archway remained. Lan wiped his sleeve over his forehead. The unlocking had taken more from him than he'd thought possible. An instant of fear flashed through him.

Was he as powerful as he thought? Did this multiple spell hold traps of which he was unaware? Had he committed too much of his power too soon? Gut-wrenching terror chewed at his self-confidence, but he dared not admit it. Not in front of Kiska.

"Let's not tarry. Our destiny lies in wait beyond."

With more confidence than he felt, he walked forward. Lan's eyes blinked as he passed under the stone archway. A slight electric tingle of spell had not been driven off, but it was a minor annoyance. He flicked it away as if it were nothing more than a buzzing insect.

He entered the chamber containing Claybore's legs.

"There they are!" cried Kiska. "Claybore's lost limbs."

Lan restrained her. She tried to bolt forward and seize the beaten copper coffins holding those legs.

"The exterior protective spells are gone. Others remain. How else could those legs stay preserved?"

"Claybore is immortal. His parts are, too."

Lan reeled at the notion. For whatever reason, this had never occurred to him. He studied the twin coffins and saw the spells woven through the fabric of the metal and flesh within and knew that Kiska was right. The spells the mage Lirory had placed on the legs bound them to this time and place; preservation was accomplished on a more fundamental level, one fraught with magics that even Lan did not pretend to understand.

"They can be destroyed," he said, more to maintain the fiction of his superiority than anything else. Showing ignorance in front of Kiska bothered him more than he cared to admit.

"Of course they can be destroyed," came a voice all too familiar from previous encounters. The words did not sound against air as others' words might, but echoed from within the head. Claybore spoke directly from mind to mind. "You ought to know that my parts are not invincible. After all, you left my skin in a puddle of protoplasm from your spells."

"I wondered when you would come," said Lan, turning to face Claybore. The sorcerer stood under the archway so recently swept clean of its guardian spells. His human torso and arms were carried on a magically powered mechanical contrivance of metal struts and spinning cogwheels that now showed the ravages of continual battle. The inhuman fleshless skull, however, betrayed Lan Martak's successes the most clearly. Cracks had appeared and the lower jaw was missing. For all the damage wrought to the bone, the dark pits still glowed with the red, manic fury of Claybore's death beams.

"I waited for you to tire yourself, to do the work for me."

"I am not tired, Claybore."

"You kid yourself, then," said Claybore, laughing. His mocking gestures angered Lan, who watched as the sorcerer came into the chamber. The arms took up a defensive pose, ready to subvert any spell Lan might cast.

Lan savored this moment. Claybore might decry his skills,

but Lan knew deep within how he had grown as a mage. Claybore was not only wrong, he was defeated and didn't know it. Lan Martak *felt* the power on him. He could not lose. He faced his destiny.

"This after you've told me it's possible to destroy your parts? Kiska was wrong. The parts are not immortal. The whole might be, but not the parts."

"Immortality rests with all the parts, but that doesn't mean the segments cannot be destroyed," said Claybore. "Left alone, they will survive for all eternity."

"Consummate magics will destroy them," said Lan, almost gloating now.

"Terrill tried and failed. He paid the penalty for dismembering me."

"I'm better than Terrill."

The chalk white skull tipped sideways, the eye sockets taking on a blackness darker than space. The area around the nose hole became riddled with cracks as magical forces mounted. Claybore's skull disintegrated a bit more under each attack. Lan felt confident that he would turn the skull into dust before the day was out.

"You think so?" mocked Claybore.

"I *feel* it."

"You're a fool. You're a fool I have manipulated for my own ends for some time. You cannot win. You don't even understand what stakes we play for."

"Conquest. Power."

"Yes, that," said Claybore, stopping beside the copper coffin cradling his left leg. "And more. Power is worthless useless it is used. After you've conquered a few thousand worlds, what then? With immortality, mere power is not enough."

"What else can there be?" asked Lan, wondering if this were a trick to gull him into vulnerability.

"Godhood! Not only power but the worship of all living beings. Their birth, their death, every instant in between ruled totally—by me! For millennia there has been no true god because I imprisoned the Resident of the Pit."

Lan's agile mind worked over the details and filled in gaps. It all fit a pattern. Whether or not what was being said was true he didn't know, but it could well be. Terrill had been the Resident's pawn in the battle against Claybore, but what was the nature of that conflict?

It had to be for the godhood Claybore mentioned. The sorcerer had dueled the reigning deity—the Resident of the Pit—and had somehow gained the upper hand. But the Resident fought back with Terrill as his principal weapon. Lacking full power, the Resident had not destroyed Claybore, but Terrill had succeeded in scattering the bodily parts along the Road.

"You get a glimmering of the truth," said Claybore. "I failed to destroy the Resident and ended up dismembered. But the Resident was unable to regain godhood because I hold him imprisoned. A stalemate lasting centuries."

"One which is drawing to a close," said Lan. "Regaining your legs will give you the power to finally destroy the Resident. After all this time, you will be able to kill a deity."

"Yes," came the sibilant acknowledgment. "And in the universe ruled by the god Claybore, there will be no further use for fools such as you. Prepare to die, Lan Martak."

The spell Claybore cast exploded like the heart of a sun, blinding him, leaving him cut free of all his senses and floating through empty infinity.

Spinning through space blinded and deaf, totally without senses, had startled him—but fear wasn't his response. He fought and found within himself the right ways of countering Claybore's attack.

He whirled back, still facing Claybore. No time had elapsed. The wild flight had been entirely illusory—but ever so real while he was caught up in the spell.

"A petty trick," he said, knowing how Claybore had done it. "Good-bye."

The spell he cast contained elements of the most powerful spells he was capable of controlling. The invisible web caught at Claybore and further cracked the skull, a piece falling to the stone floor. Lan tightened and the magics spilled over from the edge of his control and eroded away the coffin immediately in front of Claybore.

That almost proved his undoing.

The left leg, freed of its magical bindings, kicked out of the copper coffin and balanced in a mockery of life on the floor. The sight of the dismembered leg moving of its own volition startled Lan into relaxing his attack.

Claybore's riposte came in an unexpected fashion. The leg hopped forward and kicked straight for Lan's groin. The physical pain meant little to Lan; the shock of seeing the leg attack allowed cracks to develop in his own defenses.

Claybore entered that breach easily. The spells used by the mage beat at Lan's every vulnerable point. He was forced backward, driven to the wall. The inner core on which he relied came to his aid, giving him the respite to reform his defenses.

All the while, the ghastly leg continued to hop forward and kick at him.

"See, Martak? All of me wants to see you die," said Claybore. "And you will—you will die as only an immortal can. You will live forever and be in complete pain for all eternity. Nothing will save you. You will cry in the dark for surcease and never find it. You will die, not in body but in mind. Die, Martak, die!"

Lan couldn't stop the surging attack, but he deflected it enough to keep from succumbing. Knowing his strength was nowhere near adequate to destroy Claybore as he'd thought, cunning took over. Lan Martak turned aside the assault and redirected it to the hopping, kicking leg.

"No!" came the shriek as Claybore realized what was happening.

His leg vanished in a sizzling cloud of greasy black smoke, lost forever.

"Your skin is gone. I have your tongue. Now your left leg is destroyed. Who is losing, Claybore?"

Lan twisted away as heat destroyed the other copper coffin. Droplets of molten metal seared his skin, raised blisters, burned like a million ants devouring his flesh. The other leg bounded free of its vaporized coffin and went hopping toward Claybore.

Lan tried to stop the right leg and found the other sorcerer's spells prevented it. Leg and torso would soon be reunited. What power would this give Claybore? Lan didn't want to find out.

"You can't stop me, Martak," gloated Claybore. "You had your chance. You've failed."

"Aren't you the one failing, Claybore? Where's your left leg? It's gone. Completely destroyed. The other soon will be."

"Never!"

Lan sent out tangling spells to numb the nerves in the leg. They failed. The leg did not live in the same way other animate creatures did. He hurled fireballs and sent elementals and opened pits and still he failed to prevent the inexorable movement of the leg as it hopped toward Claybore.

Every spell he wove sapped him of that much more strength. Lan realized with a sick feeling that Claybore was growing stronger. When the leg rejoined, his power would be supreme.

"All the universe will be mine to rule," came Claybore's mocking words, so soft and sibilant that they were almost a whisper. "More than ruling, all the peoples of those worlds will worship me. I shall reign forever!"

"Won't that pall on you?" gasped out Lan. He countered a nerve-numbing spell, started a chant of his own to renew his attack. Power slipped from him like a dropped cloak. Grabbing at it only caused it to slide away faster.

"Ask me in a million years."

"You'll ruin worlds."

"Yes."

"You don't care. You owe it to the people you'll rule not to harm them."

"Why?" Then Claybore's laughter echoed in Lan's skull. "Your tone has changed, Martak. Now you're trying to invest me with a conscience. You're admitting I have won. It is apparent, isn't it?"

"Yes," Lan grated out—but he had one last spell to try. Lan had not dared use it for fear of releasing energies beyond his control.

Lan began the magical summoning motions with his fingers. The air twisted into improbable shapes before him. The arcane words he chanted formed colored threads in the midst of the writhing mass. But one element of the spell was missing. He reached forth, summoned the dancing mote of light that had become his familiar, and sent it directly into the vortex to supply power.

Power!

The virtually uncontrolled spell burst forth with more vehemence than Lan had anticipated—or Claybore expected.

The sorcerer screamed as his leg froze in midhop and fell lifeless to the stone floor. His rejoined arms began twitching spastically, and Lan watched in fascination as the Kinetic Sphere, Claybore's very heart, began pushing outward from his chest. But the potent spell was not without effect on Lan. His mouth turned metallic, and his tongue began to glow hotter and hotter. This spell affected *all* of Claybore's bodily parts and that included the tongue ripped from the other mage's mouth.

"You can't do this!" shrieked Claybore. The ghastly apparition of the sorcerer leaped and cavorted about, dodging unseen menace. The cracks in the skull deepened until Lan wondered how it held together. With the jaw bone already gone, Claybore's visage turned even more gruesome with every passing moment.

Lan found himself unable to speak, but the sensation of victory assuaged that. Claybore was becoming wrapped in the spell and would soon lie as numbed on the floor as his left leg. No longer even kicking, the leg presented no menace at all. Its magics were contained. And Claybore would be soon, also.

Lan blinked in surprise when all the magical attacks against him suddenly ceased. His tongue still burned, but that was the product of his own conjuring.

"Giving up so easily, Claybore?" he croaked out. Then Lan saw what the sorcerer did. The attack hadn't lessened, it had shifted.

Kiska k'Adesina writhed on the floor, face blue from the

spells cutting off her air. Her body arched violently as if her back would snap, then she flopped onto her belly and fingers cut into stone as she tried to escape Claybore's vicious magical punishment.

"Stop it!" cried Lan.

Without thinking, he directed his full power to shielding the woman from Claybore. The instant his attack on Claybore stopped, the disembodied sorcerer countered.

"You can't let her come to harm, can you, Martak?" chided Claybore. "You love her. You *must* protect her. You have to. She means more than your own life, doesn't she?"

"No," said Lan. The weakness of his reply told him everything. He did love Kiska k'Adesina, his sworn enemy, the woman who hated him with an obsession bordering on insanity; he loved her.

The geas controlled him.

"I see it in your face. Defend her. Keep her from harm."

Claybore's spells trapped the woman on the floor like a bug with a pin through it. She gasped for breath, twisted about as joints snapped and limbs turned in ways never intended. Lan watched in rapt horror as Claybore broke her physically with his powerful spells.

But if he protected Kiska adequately, he left himself open to attack. One or the other of them he might defend, but not both of them.

"She dies, Martak. Your lover dies."

The desolation welling up within Lan couldn't be expressed. He had no true love for Kiska. She had tried to kill him on more occasions than he could count, yet he did love her. Irrationally, without any regard for common sense, Lan loved Kiska.

"Look at her pain, Martak. I really don't want to do this to one who has been such a loyal follower, but it gives me some practice. When I become a true god I think I shall do this every day."

Lan gambled everything on forming one last spell to hurl every spark of energy he had directly at Claybore. Stun Claybore, stop the torture Kiska felt.

The bolt lashed forth with such intensity the rock walls

turned viscid and flowed in sluggish, molten streams. The dancing light mote guided the tip of this energy blast directly for Claybore's skull. The sorcerer staggered back, his metallic legs beginning to melt under the onslaught. But the reaction was not that which Lan expected. Claybore was being driven to the wall and yet an aura of triumph surrounded him.

Lan jerked about, trying to discover the reason. He saw his friends entering. The giant spider Krek lumbered forward, his eight legs ungainly in the confines of the tunnel and chamber. Large brown eyes took in all that happened. Behind Krek came dark-haired Inyx, sword drawn and an expression of bloodlust etched on her handsome face. She and Lan had been through much together as they walked the Road, and his current attitudes about Kiska and the single-minded drive he displayed for stopping Claybore weren't going to deter her from helping him in his moment of need. Just behind the fierce warrior woman stood Ducasien, the man from Inyx's home world, the one to whom she had turned when Lan was unable to comfort her.

"Stop her!" came Krek's voice. Lan ventured a quick glance to one side and saw Kiska k'Adesina rising up, dagger in hand. The dagger was aimed straight for his back.

As long as he maintained the spell against Claybore, Lan couldn't move, couldn't defend himself against physical attack. Even worse was the sight of the woman he loved trying to kill him, as if she still plotted with Claybore for his downfall.

Inyx rushed forward, her quick, strong hand gripping Kiska's wrist and twisting at the last possible instant. Lan felt hot steel rake over his back. Thick streams of blood gushed forth, but the wound was messier than it was dangerous.

But the shock of seeing the woman he was magically forced to love attempt to kill him broke the continuity of his spell. Claybore began worming free of the attack.

"Come," the sorcerer beckoned. "Come to me!"

The leg twitched and kicked and bobbed until it again hopped across the chamber. Lan's power waned; he was unable to cope with Inyx and Kiska fighting, the spell he launched against Claybore and the countering spell the sorcerer returned, and the sight of the leg hopping to rejoin the body.

"Krek," he moaned. "The leg. Stop it!"

Krek's huge front limb reached out and batted away the leg, sending it into the far wall. Flesh hissed slightly as it touched rock already turned molten from other spells.

"The heat. Oh, my precious fur is smouldering," cried the spider.

"Never mind that. Stop the leg from reaching Claybore."

Lan's words needed more conviction to get the spider to move. The way the man's tongue burned within his mouth told him that his own enervating spell had been turned against him. Claybore's cunning played on his every weakness, his every mistake.

But if Krek was unable to move, the gnome's leader Broit Heresler and his few surviving clansmen did act. The gnomes, who called this hollowed mountain their home, rushed into the chamber, spades and picks cutting and hacking at the leg. The limb tried valiantly to defend itself against the tiny chunks being taken out of it, but there were too many gnomes attacking.

Claybore cursed, tried to magically destroy them, and found himself overextended. He dared not relent in his attack on Lan; to do so meant his own demise. But he needed his leg and the gnomes prevented it from rejoining him.

"Bring out the water," Broit called. Others of the gravedigger clan rolled huge barrels into the room.

"You can't do that!" shrieked Claybore.

They threw acid water onto the leg. Flesh smouldered and turned putrescent. Soon, only the bare leg bones remained, and they were easily hammered into dust by the gnomes.

"You've lost, Claybore," said Lan. "Stop your drive for power now. We can work out some sort of truce."

"Truce? You fool! You don't understand. I've tasted ultimate power. I can't turn away from it. I can't share it."

The sorcerer lay in a heap on the ground, his metallic legs destroyed and his own legs unreachable now. Lan Martak had magically blasted the one leg and the other was little more than bonemeal in a paste of acid water on the floor.

Claybore reached up and touched the spot on his chest where the Kinetic Sphere pinkly pulsed.

"You will find this victory fleeting, Martak," promised Claybore. The sorcerer's entire body blinked out of existence. The sorcerer walked the Road.

"You killed him!" cried Broit Heresler, jumping up and down, his bandy legs quivering with excitement.

"He shifted worlds," said Lan in a tired voice. "We stopped him from regaining either of his legs, but he still walks the Road, plotting and planning."

A strangled sound came to the mage's ears. Lan spun and saw Inyx with her fingers firmly wrapped around Kiska's throat. The dark-haired woman slowly choked the life from her victim.

"Inyx, no!" he cried. Ducasien placed a hand on Lan's shoulder to restrain him. Lan cast a minor spell that hurled Ducasien across the room. A second spell sent Inyx after him, leaving Kiska alone and gasping for air on the floor. He went to her and knelt, cradling her head in his lap.

Emotions boiled within Lan. He hated her for all she had done. She was insane, a cold-blooded murderer. And he loved her. He had to protect her at all costs.

"Lan Martak," came Krek's voice, "she attempted to stab you in the back. You saw. You know of her treachery."

"I love her," he choked out. His heart leaped with joy when he saw her muddy brown eyes flicker open and focus on him. Lan read only hatred blazing up at him and it didn't matter. He loved her.

He had to. That was the curse laid upon him.

"Good riddance," snarled Kiska k'Adesina. She stood close beside Lan Martak on the mountaintop. The circle of energy surrounding them held the acid rain at bay and gave them a clear view of the tiny procession wending its way across the barren plain to the graveyard. Lan watched and felt a coldness inside grow until he wanted to scream. Inyx gone. Krek gone. His friends had abandoned him because he was unable to break free of Claybore's spell binding him so tightly—so cunningly!—to Kiska. He didn't want them to leave, yet his actions had driven them off.

There'd be no more of Krek's odd observations on life and the worlds they explored together. Inyx would no longer be there to comfort him or defend his back during battle.

The thought of Inyx in Ducasien's arms sent rivers of hot tears rolling down his cheeks.

Lan Martak clenched his fists and shook with emotion.

"You don't need them. You have me. What were they, anyhow? A slut and an overgrown bug. You love me, Lan my darling. We can rule together."

"Be quiet," he said. Kiska only laughed at him, knowing his impotence in dealing with her.

The cenotaph blinked open and glowed a pale yellow. Lan watched the magics that linked one world to another begin to flow. First one brighter spot, then another, and finally a third and last. Inyx. Ducasien. Krek. Gone.

All that remained on this world was the burning ground where the rains washed over the stone.

"Claybore must be destroyed," he said.

"Yes, my love," came Kiska's mocking words.

Lan Martak clapped his hands and summoned newfound power to shift worlds without a cenotaph or the Kinetic Sphere. He didn't need Inyx or Krek. Claybore would be stopped. He'd show them.

A second clap of his hands prepared the world-spanning bridge of magic.

He would stop Claybore and rule a million worlds.

On the third clap of his hands, only barren rock showed where he and Kiska had stood. They now walked a lush, green meadow on a world distant in space and time.

CHAPTER TWO

The skies split above Lan Martak's head. Gone were the
heavy, leaden clouds that had sent their torrents of
acid-laced rain down on the mountain kingdom of Yerrary.
Replacing them came rainbows blazing through the spec-
trum, touching on all the colors and adding new ones Lan
had never before seen. Then these, too, vanished and melted
into swirling, churning whites and greys that took form,
lurched out at him, and dissipated. Dizzy, stumbling, he
fell forward into ...

    ... green.

    ... soft.

    ... summer.

Lan Martak blinked and smiled slowly as he surveyed
this new world. Traveling through the cenotaphs had always
produced a disjointed sensation, a falling that ended with
an abrupt stop. His new magics gave him more control over
the transition between worlds. Claybore might require the
Kinetic Sphere to perform his world-stepping, but Lan now
went him one better. Only a simple uttered spell gave him
access to all the worlds along the Cenotaph Road!

"This is much nicer," said Kiska k'Adesina. "That other world was too dreary." Lan looked at her, empty inside. No emotion sprang forth when he deigned to notice the brown-haired woman. She was his avowed enemy, and he felt nothing.

Lan almost rejoiced in this neutrality. He tried to coax more of it into play. He knew full well that Claybore had placed a geas on him, but no spells or chant at Lan's command removed it. Kiska would be a millstone around his neck and, one day when he least expected it, that weight would carry him under the surface and drown him. If only he could remove her before then!

He wanted to. Deep inside he knew a provocation great enough would give him the strength to sunder Claybore's geas. He tried to bring it forth. Intellectually he knew that she was responsible for untold suffering on a dozen planets. She commanded Claybore's grey-clad legions and subjugated entire worlds in the dismembered mage's name. Lan had no love for Kiska k'Adesina.

And yet he did. The man choked as the geas asserted itself. Lan fought the churnings deep within, the love tinglings that mocked him and his most adroit spells. He shook off the sexual urges and concentrated on the world spread before him.

"Summer," he said. A light, humid breeze caressed his face and warmed flesh that had been chilled on another world just a step—and incalculable distances—away. He sucked in a lungful of the air and tasted freshness, the heady fragrance of flowers in bloom, the slight decays of forest mulch that meant renewed growth for other plants and trees. He closed his eyes and heard the insistent hum of insects. Lan batted away a few of the more eager bugs as they landed on his forehead and neck.

Kiska gripped his arm and broke the serene mood. "Look, Lan, there. Below. In the valley."

Reluctantly, he focused his gaze on the terrain stretching out from beneath his feet. Even without his magics, he knew what it was like being a god. Simply standing and looking at this fair world caused the feelings to rise within.

"Claybore's legions," he said. Twin lines of grey marched along the riverbanks. From their formation he saw they had no fear of attack. This was their world and they ruled it totally. Lan moved so that he could study Kiska's reaction. She was, after all, a commander in Claybore's army. The small smirk on the woman's face told him what he needed to know. These troops spelled danger for him.

But how?

Did the trap lie in avoiding contact with the troops, or in openly confronting them? Should he flee now before they spotted him or should he attack while surprise was in his favor? Endless possibilities flowed through his mind, like clear water across a river rock. Lan found no answer.

"Well?" demanded Kiska. "What are you going to do?"

"What would you have me do? There are hundreds of them. I can hardly fight each and every one." He placed his hand on the sword still dangling from his belt. It had been a long while since he'd drawn the weapon. His battles had become more magical.

"A sword?" she said scornfully. "Use your magic. Slay all of them with a fireball."

"You want me to alert Claybore? Any use of magic will allow him to home in on me."

"Why not?" Kiska asked. "You can defeat him." The sly look in her eye told Lan that she believed otherwise. She tried to lure him into a not too subtle trap.

"We go," he said. "Down the other side of the hill."

"Where? Where are we going? Are we to wander aimlessly, looking for pretty stones and interesting plants? Or do you have a plan?"

"No plan," Lan said. Kiska moved closer to him, but he shrugged off her embrace. The man wanted nothing more than to be alone with his own thoughts—to be alone physically. But the geas prevented him from chasing her away. The mere thought of Kiska k'Adesina being out of his sight caused him to shiver uncontrollably and break into a sweat.

They walked down the far side of the hill until they came

to a tributary to the river flowing down the far valley. Here
they made camp, Lan looking for easy game to catch. He
started to stun a small, furry creature with a spell, then held
back at the last instant. Instead, he clubbed it with a rock.
The spell, no matter how trivial, would alert Claybore to
his presence. Lan's instincts told him to keep hidden for as
long as he could, learn Claybore's weaknesses, find his own
strengths, and explore the odd vision given him on the other
world.

The Pillar of Night, Claybore had called it.

The memory blurred for Lan, something quite unusual.
The magics bound within that towering spire of the blackest
stone provided the key to destroying Claybore. All Lan had
to do was learn the secret of the Pillar of Night. He snorted
and shook his head. Simple. Or it ought to be for one who
had pretensions of becoming a god.

Lan swung his crude stone hand axe and clubbed a second
animal. He carried them back to camp, where Kiska had
laid a small fire.

"Clean them," he said, dropping the animals at her feet.

"Later," she said in a husky voice. She stood and ap-
proached him. Lan couldn't move. He needed her. He had
to have her.

She came into his arms and they kissed deeply. The
revulsion welling inside Lan made him want to gag. He
didn't. He felt her hot breath against his lips, his cheek, his
ear, his throat, lower. Lan's heart almost exploded as Kiska
coaxed even more from him. They sank to the soft turf
together and made love.

Weakness boiled inside the man. The invincible mage
felled by a woman he hated—and had to love. Lan drifted
off to sleep, wondering where Inyx and Krek were. And if
Inyx were locked in Ducasien's arms. The sleep, when it
came, was not restful.

Lan Martak awoke, hand on sword. The darkness cloaking
the tiny glade told him that it was well after sundown,
perhaps as late as midnight. The stars wheeled through the

sky in unfamiliar patterns and sounds totally unique told
him of strange beasts stalking and being stalked.

One sound echoing through the forest brought Lan to his
feet. He recognized the whisper of metal against leather,
the feet marching, the movement of soldiers.

"Kiska," he said, shaking the woman awake. He wanted
to leave her, but the spell forced him to warn her. "We have
company."

"Ummm," she said, rubbing her eyes. Those brown eyes
snapped wide open when she saw Lan with sword already
in hand. No fear showed through, but Kiska tensed. "What
is it?"

He silently motioned for her to follow. She gathered their
few belongings and trailed behind, making no attempt to
move quietly. To Lan and his forest-trained senses, she
made more noise than all of Claybore's grey-clad soldiers.

Lan fought down the urge to use a simple scrying spell.
To know the troop numbers, their movement, their positions, would make eluding them so much easier. But he
dared not betray his position. In the far distance he "saw"
magics stirring, a dim, unsettling sensation for him. Lan
had yet to identify the source as Claybore's magics, but if
Lan spotted the use of arcane lore this easily, Claybore
would be able to "see" him, also.

Surprise, Lan thought grimly, was his only ally. And a
fickle one it was, at best.

He peered around the charred bole of a lightning-struck
tree and saw the broken formation of soldiers advancing.
They crept forward in waves, the soldiers behind protecting
those advancing. Only when the new terrain was adequately
scouted did those behind move forward to reconnoiter further.

"They're armed with bows," Kiska said. "An odd choice
for this world."

"What do you mean?" Lan demanded.

"Oh, nothing," the woman said. Even in the dim light
filtering through the forest's canopy of broad green leaves,
Lan saw the smirk on Kiska's lips.

"Make any sound to attract their attention and I'll kill you," Lan said.

Kiska laughed at him, the laughter drifting through the forest and alerting the man on the closest end of the combat line. The grey-clad soldier spun and motioned to the man next to him.

Lan gripped his sword hilt until his fingers turned white. He shook himself and then started off through the forest at a breakneck clip. The mage hardly cared if Kiska kept up with his pace or not. He wanted to eliminate her with a single sword thrust—and he couldn't. The fires of the geas burned the brighter within him now as his anger grew. The spell laid upon him always proved more powerful than his own will. Cursing, damning Claybore for doing this to him, damning Kiska and all the grey-clads, he found a rocky knoll poking up out of the gently grassed forest on which to make his stand.

"They come for you, Lan my love," mocked Kiska.

"Go on, kill me now," he said. He stood, sword point lowered. Kiska k'Adesina pulled forth her dagger and started to obey. She wanted to kill him; with all her heart and black soul, she would!

The dagger danced about in her trembling hand. She swallowed hard and sank to her knees. "I can't," she muttered. "I can't!"

Lan looked at her and, in that moment, shared the frustration. The spell Claybore had wrought bound them both. Whatever the disembodied mage had in mind, the time was not yet right for the trap to spring. Lan Martak recognized the deadliness of having Kiska beside him and could do little to prevent it. If anything, knowing Claybore's spell would suddenly erupt into violence and death—and not knowing the exact instant—made the waiting all the more excruciating.

"Defend yourself," Lan said. "These grey-clads will kill anyone with me."

"No, they . . . won't," she said, unsure.

The first arrow barely missed Kiska's right arm. She

jerked back and stared in disbelief at the feathered shaft buried in the soft turf.

"Fight or die," Lan said. His heart raced now, as much for his own safety as for the woman's. Damn Claybore!

A flight of arrows from the shadows caused Lan to drop behind a stump for cover. He reached out and pulled Kiska flat. The second barrage from the soldiers was instantly followed by six men with drawn swords.

"A spell!" Kiska cried. "Fry them with a fireball!"

Lan's blade slashed across the first man's eyes, sending him reeling back into the ranks with blood fountaining. Another thrust to the throat slipped under a sergeant's gorget and penetrated the Adam's apple. A heavy boot broke another's wrist.

"Fight!" Lan cried to Kiska. "Would you see me slaughtered here and now?"

"Yes," she hissed, but the woman was on her feet, dagger seeking target after target. Claybore's spell still cut both ways. Lan and Kiska might hate one another, but they were tightly bound together. Until that indeterminate time arrived when Claybore's diabolical trap would be sprung, Kiska had to fight to save her "lover," just as Lan fought to save Kiska.

Another half-dozen arrows winged toward Lan. Reflex action caused him to use a fire spell; the arrows burst into flame and turned to ash inches from his chest. He lunged and caught another soldier on the upper arm, putting him out of the fray.

"How many of them are there?" moaned Kiska. She was covered with blood—Lan couldn't tell how much was hers—and obviously weakened. She had retrieved a fallen sword and used it, but the greys still swarmed from the safety of the woods. Only the slight rise gave Lan and Kiska a fighting advantage.

"Too many," said Lan. He didn't want to use another spell, but he had no other choice. Alerting Claybore of his presence was not as immediately dangerous as dying on the sword point of one of Claybore's soldiers.

Lan's lips moved imperceptibly, the spell forming. The full power of the tongue resting within his mouth would be sent forth at the proper instant.

"They all attack!" cried Kiska.

"*Die!*" Lan commanded, using the Voice.

Fourteen of the grey-clads stopped, stiffened, then dropped their weapons. For the span of three heartbeats not a single soldier moved. Then they slumped to the ground like rows of wheat being harvested.

"Such power," Kiska said softly, looking at Lan. "Claybore's tongue is mightier than all their swords."

Lan tried forming the spell again, this time directed at Kiska. He failed, as he had known he would.

"Claybore now knows I have come after him," said Lan. "I had hoped for more time to study this world."

"You can see the Pillar of Night?" asked the woman. She shoved the sword into the soft dirt and wiped it free of blood. Kiska searched through the ranks of the fallen soldiers until she found a sword-belt that fit her. She draped it around her waist, the sword tugging down and swinging at her left side.

"What do you know of it?" asked Lan.

"Nothing," she said blithely, enjoying the torment it caused Lan. "Claybore mentioned it once or twice. That's all."

He knew Kiska lied. She knew more than a casual mention by the dismembered sorcerer. But what?

Lan closed his eyes and "looked" around him. A pale glow pulsed from a spot a few hours' walk away. The light warmed Lan, made him smile in fond recollection. Here was an ally. Perhaps not one overly dependable, but an ally nonetheless. Without a word to his companion, Lan started through the forest toward the green beacon of magic.

"Here," said Kiska with some distaste. She held out the kicking, clawing badger for Lan to take.

"Do it," he said, pointing. "Toss the beast into the well."

Kiska obeyed. The badger twisted and tried to savage

her hand, but it was too late. Falling, the creature dwindled
to a point of brown and then vanished into inky darkness.
For some time nothing happened. Then the absolute blackness within the well began to churn and move, to take form,
to rise.

"What have you conjured?" Kiska said, backing away
from the lip of the well.

"I should have tossed you into the pit," Lan said.

Inchoate space pulsed with life now and a somber voice
said, "Welcome, Lan Martak. You have arrived, as I knew
you would."

"Where is Claybore?" asked Lan.

"On this world," came the Resident of the Pit's sly answer.

"How do I fight him?"

"With all your skills."

Lan pondered. The Resident always answered questions
honestly, but obliquely.

"How has Claybore imprisoned you?" Lan asked.

"There is no answer for this, Lan Martak," came the
baleful answer. "If I knew the exact spells, I might free
myself of them."

"You are, after all, a god," said Lan.

"A deposed one," said the Resident of the Pit, "and one
willing to die. Eternity is too long for me. I have been
trapped within this pit for thousands of years."

"The pit?" asked Kiska. "It opens onto other worlds? I
saw one such as this back in Yerrary."

"I," said the Resident, "am everywhere and nowhere.
On every world there are wells similar to this one, but none
worships me now. Claybore has thwarted me."

Kiska laughed. "I know you now. Terrill was your pawn,
wasn't he? He tried to free you from the Pillar of Night and
failed."

"True," said the Resident.

Lan frowned. He walked in circles around the mouth of
the pit, occasionally looking into the writhing mass of in-
substantial blackness trapped within.

"Am I also your pawn?" asked Lan.

"I aid you in whatever manner I can," said the Resident. "I will tell you this, and nothing more because of the spells binding me: the Pillar of Night is both Claybore's strength and his weakness."

"I must destroy it?"

The whirlpool of blackness spun, then slackened in speed, dipped back into the pit and vanished, shadow melting into shadow.

Lan's frustration rose. It always proved thus with the Resident of the Pit. Vague hints, nothing definite, warnings too general to be meaningful.

"Now that you've enjoyed my fair world," came Claybore's taunting words, "it is time for you to leave. Goodbye, Martak!"

The attack came from all directions at once. Lan fell to his knees under the onslaught of magics. Spells of mind-numbing complexity worked to burn away his flesh. His eyes expanded within his skull and threatened to explode. His genitals itched. Sounds shrill and deafening assaulted his ears even as bass vibrations shook his internal organs, churning one against the other. He clapped hands over his ears and screwed shut his eyes to protect himself.

And the attack grew.

"Stop!" he commanded, the Voice ringing from his lips. The magical tongue burned in his mouth and tasted foul with its metallic tang. But the single word caused the slightest of cracks in the battering ram of spells Claybore used against him.

That small crack widened as Lan regained his senses. He twisted magically and stood in relative calm.

Both mages surrounded themselves with protective bubbles of intricate, ever-changing magics.

"You have progressed," said Claybore. "Even in the brief months since we parted company, you have learned much."

Lan said nothing. To Claybore it might have been months. For him it was mere hours. Time flowed differently between the worlds—and Lan realized for the first time that

Claybore's Kinetic Sphere gave the other mage instant translation between worlds. Lan's self-taught spells were of a different nature and might have produced the time delay.

He studied Claybore and saw that the sorcerer's arms produced new and different patterns of glowing air before him. Reds flowed into greens only to burst into brilliant white pinwheels that sent sparks in all directions. Lan wished he had prevented Claybore from recovering his arms; the added power in Claybore's conjurations was instantly apparent.

"You have repaired your legs," Lan said.

Claybore did not glance down. The fleshless skull atop his shoulder lacked eyes. In the deep sockets ruby light swirled about, waiting to form death beams. The skull's lower jaw had been destroyed, but the cracks Lan had caused in the white bone had been patched.

"A master mechanician labored for weeks to rebuild my legs. They are better than ever." Claybore flexed one of the metal wonders. Lan saw the bright points of magic powering the legs. He snuffed out one of the spots and Claybore almost fell.

"Damn you!" snarled the sorcerer. The power point returned and Claybore straightened.

"Let's go on a trip, shall we?" asked Lan, his voice deceptively mild. *"Now!"* This time he put all the prodigious power of the Voice into his spell.

The pair of them tumbled through the air, spinning and turning about as magics carried them aloft.

Lan's view of the world widened and what he saw he liked. It struck him as a crime that one such as Claybore could befoul such a bucolic place with his presence. Claybore would not rule this world—or any other! He kept the other sorcerer off balance by shifting the force of gravity, slackening in places and augmenting in others.

"A trick, Martak, but not good enough." Claybore's fingers wiggled and new patterns of burning light shone forth. The tumbling ceased and they rocketed around the world, moving faster and faster until Lan fought for breath. The rushing air burned at his clothes, made his tunic smoulder, set the leather grips of his sword ablaze.

"Cool!" he commanded, the Voice again producing the desired results. The friction-fed fires died as light breezes wafted past him. Lan Martak breathed normally now and began building an assault against Claybore that combined every deadly spell he knew into one vicious, icepick-slender thrust.

Claybore screeched inhumanly as the magical dagger sank deep. The Kinetic Sphere turned bright red and began melting within the sorcerer's chest. Claybore begged for release. Lan refused.

"I hadn't thought I had the power to defeat you, Claybore," he said. "I was wrong. This is the moment of your death."

"I cannot die," grated out Claybore. "I am immortal. *We* are immortal."

"Terrill found your weakness. So have I." Like a small boy pulling the wings off an unwilling insect, Lan Martak plucked the Kinetic Sphere from Claybore's chest and sent it spinning across the heavens. The cavity where it had beat heartlike in the other mage's chest began to putrefy. The edges of flesh in the torso gleamed with pinkish fluids that dripped into space. Lan pressed his attack even more.

"You have enslaved millions. You would enslave and torture more. I will stop you. I, Lan Martak!"

The power was on him. Lan felt it building up and flowing like a river through his body. He could not fail. He was invincible. He was immortal. He was a god!

"Look!" sobbed Claybore.

The sleek black column rose from the plains below them. Lan blinked. This had to be the Pillar of Night. The spikes ringing the ebon top of the shaft rotated slowly as he watched. And something stirred within him. The Resident of the Pit had said this was Claybore's strength and his weakness.

How? What was it? What did it mean?

The distraction proved Lan's undoing. Even as the sight of the Pillar of Night captivated him, he felt his spells weakening.

"Enjoy eternity, Martak," came the sorcerer's distant, haunting words. "Enjoy the nothingness between worlds, for it will be your home forever!"

Lan Martak turned and took a single step forward into . . . ghostly whiteness.

CHAPTER THREE

Rainbows filled her universe. The distant roar Inyx always experienced when shifting from one world to the next using the cenotaph seemed muted this time, but she paid it little attention. This was the first time in many months she had walked the Road without Lan beside her.

The dark-haired woman didn't know if she liked that or not.

"This looks fair enough, even for ones like ourselves," said Inyx's companion. Ducasien stretched mightily and yawned, rubbing his stubbled chin and walking about the small graveyard. They had emerged on a hillside looking down on a barren expanse stretching off to a meandering river, its banks bursting from the spring runoffs.

"There's promise in the air," she agreed.

Behind her came a low moan and a rattling noise. She turned to see the giant spider Krek emerging from the cenotaph. Huge mandibles moved aside the stone coffin lid and as easily moved it back when the arachnid was fully transported into this world.

"What's wrong, Krek?" she asked.

"Oh, friend Inyx, it is terrible, so positively terrible. I ache all over. My exoskeleton is in terrible shape. Look at the dents, the horrid gashes, even the burn marks. Burn marks! Why did I ever do such an insane thing? Why?"

"What's that?" asked Ducasien.

"Leave my lovely bride Klawn and go a'wandering along the thrice-cursed Road," answered the spider, glad to find a human willing to listen to his plight. "You have not seen gentle, petite Klawn, have you, friend Ducasien?"

"Can't say that I have," the man admitted. He frowned in confusion. Inyx caught his eye and made gestures indicating "petite" Klawn was even larger than Krek.

Krek stuck out his long, coppery-furred legs and scraped chitinous talons on the tips against a tombstone.

"Nicks. There are nicks in my talons. A disgrace. No Webmaster allows himself to deteriorate so. I shame myself. Oh, woe!"

"There, there, Krek," soothed Inyx, putting her arm around the middle pair of the spider's legs. "The acid burns will go away. Your fine fur will grow back, in time. And there's an entire world to explore. Klawn may not be here, but think of the adventure!"

"Lan Martak is not here, either," said the spider.

Inyx noted that Krek had not used his usual title of "friend" in referring to Lan.

"Lan fights battles we cannot share," she told the mountain arachnid. The woman knew she had to choose her words carefully or she'd break down and cry. "He follows his own path along the Road, and it split apart from ours."

"He was my friend and he betrayed me," moaned Krek. "What did I do to deserve such hypocrisy?"

"It wasn't your fault, old spider," spoke up Ducasien. "He plays with the magics and they are possessing him. We're better rid of him, if you ask me." The man's gaze did not waver when Inyx glared hotly at him. "Martak thinks only of himself, not you. Nor of Krek."

The accusation hurt Inyx, but she couldn't deny it. Lan had changed. Drastically. While she knew some of it had to do with the geas placed on him by Claybore, more of it came from within the man. The magical powers grew and changed his values. He had become obsessed with stopping Claybore and—what? Becoming a god? Inyx no longer mattered to him.

But he still mattered to her. A great deal.

"We can find whatever we want on this world. I feel it in my bones," said Ducasien. He placed a powerful paw of a hand on her shoulder. She smiled weakly and nodded.

"This is not my sort of place," Krek said unexpectedly. "I do like you both, I do. Believe that, friends Inyx and Ducasien. But there is a wrongness to this place that disturbs me." The spider heaved himself to his feet and lumbered about the graveyard. Krek stopped when he came to another grave marker. His talons and strong legs began pulling at the stone.

"What is it, Krek?" Inyx asked.

"Another cenotaph. Most unusual finding two in one spot. This might be a world of great heroes. Alas, I am not a hero. I am a coward, a fool, worse. I leave web and bride and wander aimlessly. I am lost."

"Krek?"

"No, friend Inyx. Let me be. A new cenotaph opens. I sense this world to be one more to my liking."

"We'll come with you . . ." Inyx started.

"No!" Krek shook all over, his head swiveling from side to side. "Stay. Explore. Find peace, if you can. I am doomed to wander, though this new world is strangely appealing to me. Farewell, friend Inyx. May your sword arm always be strong, friend Ducasien."

"Krek, wait!" Inyx started forward, but Ducasien pulled her back. Krek folded up his eight long legs and hunkered down into the exposed crypt. A dull purple haze rose from within the grave and tugged at Krek's body, pulling him to another world along the Cenotaph Road.

"Why did he do that?" Inyx asked, stunned. "He wanted to come with us. Why leave like this?"

Ducasien looked at her and then said, "Being with us will continue to remind him of all he had when you and Martak were together. Rather than face such painful memories, he prefers being alone once more. He'll be all right. From what I've seen of Krek, he's a fighter and will emerge victorious, no matter what the battle."

Inyx felt as if a piece of her had been forcibly removed and cast into another world. Losing Lan in the way she had was painful, but losing Krek, too, made it even worse. She sat and stared dry-eyed at the empty crypt where the arachnid had vanished. The grave and her insides shared one thing in common: hollowness. The woman felt drained of all emotion until only hopelessness remained.

Ducasien lifted her and held her tightly. "Krek'll be fine," he said. "Most important, *you'll* be fine. We're together now. That matters, doesn't it?"

"Yes," she said softly, her face buried in Ducasien's chest. Inyx sucked in a deep breath and pushed the man away. "What are we waiting for? There is a world to explore. Or have you changed your mind?"

Ducasien laughed and performed a courtly bow, indicating that Inyx should precede him down the hill. With forced gaiety, Inyx smiled and took the man's arm. They went down the hill, together.

"An ambush," whispered Inyx. "Not more than four."

"Six," corrected Ducasien, pointing. He indicated a rocky overhang where two more of the grey-clad soldiers hid. "They await a rider. Or more. A caravan, perhaps?"

The heavy ruts in the dusty road hinted at use by well-laden wagons. Inyx and Ducasien had traveled for more than six days before finding any sign of life. The path down from the graveyard had led to a village deader than the cemetery. Buildings had been burned to the ground within the week and not one corpse had been left behind. The other small township they had found was similarly abandoned— destroyed. Here, however, they found evidence of Claybore's grey-clad legions. A blood-stained tunic had been discarded and red-striped sleeve indicating rank in the conquering army had been ripped into bandages and then discarded, possibly when the injured had died.

The pair had trooped on, wary now for sign of Claybore's soldiers. This ambuscade gave them the first solid evidence of life on the world.

"Not much chance of a caravan," said Inyx. "They can see far enough to know if anything is kicking up dust. They wait for something—someone—else."

"Let's help whoever that is," said Ducasien, already moving to his right. Inyx waited a minute and then drifted to the left, flitting from shadow to shadow until she crouched behind one of the greys. Ducasien rose up behind his target, knife flashing in the hot sun. Inyx's victim saw and started to respond; it was the last thing he ever did. The woman rammed her dagger into his right kidney, even as her fingers pinched shut his nose and lips.

Inyx slit the throat of another before the greys' leader lifted a red-striped arm and lowered it in signal. The woman dropped into the position vacated by the dead soldier and waited.

Four men and a woman walked along the road, wary of every movement, every sound, every shadow. Inyx knew quarry when she saw it. These people had been hunted long and hard by Claybore's soldiers.

As the small group neared, the officer shouted, "Attack!"

To the officer's surprise, he found himself three men short on the ambush. Then Ducasien took out another and Inyx deftly tossed her dagger and buried the spinning blade into the chest of a fifth. The officer stood alone in the rocks, waving one arm and clinging to his sword with the other hand.

All five of the people on the road pulled out slings, whirled them around twice, and loosed their missiles. One struck the greys' leader squarely in the head. The explosion caused Inyx to flinch and turn away. She blinked in surprise. If it had been Lan attacking, she would have expected anything, but this ragtag band didn't seem the type to lavishly use magics.

"Well cast," she called to the group below. One man separated himself and stood to one side. The way he held his shoulders, the appraising look he gave her from the colorless eyes, the distance he put between himself and the others all bespoke of command.

Ducasien stepped beside her and looked down on them, saying in a low voice, "Not too awe-inspiring, are they?"

"You saw what they did to the grey-clad. There's more here than shows on the surface," Inyx said.

"Aye and you're right on that score," said the one Inyx pegged as the leader. "Come on down and join us, will you?"

"You've got good hearing," said Inyx.

"Good vision, and a mite more," said the man. "Who be you? We've not seen your likes in these parts, now have we?" He turned to the other four. The woman in the group got a far-looking experssion on her face, then slowly nodded. "Now that Julinne has passed favorably on you, be welcome with us."

"A witch?" asked Ducasien, hand still on his sword.

"Careful," Inyx cautioned. She had seen more along the Road than had her friend. Inyx remembered only too well the quaint attitudes she had carried along with her from Leponto province on her home world. It had taken many years and many different worlds to burn away the prejudices. One of the strongest had been against those wielding magics able to pry into a person's innermost thoughts.

"Well that you should be careful. Julinne's meaning you no harm, are you, my dear?"

The woman's eyes were so pale that they were virtually colorless, too. She shook her head, saying nothing.

"Julinne's not one for bandying about words. She leaves that to me. They all do now, don't you see?" The man looked from one to the next of his tight group. They relaxed as their leader spoke.

"I'm Inyx and this is Ducasien. We're travelers along the Cenotaph Road." Inyx wasn't sure the man knew of the way off his planet. Many she encountered had no inkling of interworld connections. The way Claybore recruited his troops locally fostered belief in many cultures that their ills were homegrown rather than imported.

"So I see. Julinne sees much in you to like and much that is alien." The man nodded and pointed. "You're no friends of their ilk, now are you?"

The savage grin Inyx flashed him made the man draw back. "I see that you're not," he said quickly. "I am the leader of this pathetic little group. Nowless is the name. We come from far Urm, though you're probably not quite certain where that might be, now are you?"

"No idea," said Ducasien.

"Nor," cut in Inyx, "are we sure how many you have in your 'little' band. Fifty? More?"

"Fifty?" Nowless said in mock surprise. "Now look at them, will you? Do these look to be as many as fifty? More like five."

"What about those higher up the slope? If they aren't with you, we might be in some trouble." Inyx pointed to the barren hillside. Ducasien moved a half-step closer, hand still clutching his sword. His sharp eyes began working over potential hiding spots. When he stiffened, Inyx knew he had spotted the others, too.

"I don't think there's to be any trouble," said Nowless. "You have the sense about you, eh?"

"Not like Julinne," said Inyx. "I depend on eyes and ears. You weren't talking as if you worried what we might do. One or two of those above got careless. A pebble tumbling a few feet. The scrape of leather against rock. The shadow moving where there's no life. Tiny things that all turn into something larger."

"You are a clever wench," said Nowless, a wide grin breaking out across his face. Yellowed, cracked teeth showed.

"We have a common enemy," said Ducasien, still uneasy at the large numbers of natives on the hillside. "Let's not lose sight of that."

"Friends?" demanded Nowless, squinting slightly at Ducasien.

"Friends," the man said, thrusting his sword point first into the ground.

"Were you thinking to ambush the ambushers?" asked Inyx.

"That we were. But you did such a fine job, we decided to play out a different future," said Nowless. "Would you be looking to join a fine band of the opposition? And reap some of the booty?"

"If you're opposed to Claybore's grey-clads, yes," the dark-haired woman said. Her bright blue eyes lit up with excitement. This was the sort of challenge she needed. To seek out the enemy and fight them to the death. To live by her wits. Nowless offered her the very thing she sought along the Road.

"Then it's off with us, now," said Nowless. "We have a noble mission to accomplish and the sun's going to be just right when we reach their fort."

Ducasien and Inyx walked on either side of Nowless as they continued along the dusty road for a few more miles before cutting to the west and walking into the setting sun. By the time the evening star twinkled on the horizon, they had come to a sprawling fortress dominating the mouth of a barren valley.

"How many?" asked Inyx.

"Who can say?" answered Nowless. "Even fair Julinne has trouble now and then with the seeing. She tells me of as many as a thousand within those walls." Nowless cocked his head and gave a lopsided grin. "That's about the right odds for doughty fighters such as we, don't you think?"

"We'd better get started," said Ducasien, "if we want to finish tonight. It's been weeks and weeks since I had to kill more than twenty or thirty grey-clads in a single evening."

Nowless let out a bellow of pure delight. "I knew there was a mite of humor lurking within you." Nowless pointed out the salient features of the fortress. "We can't expect to take on many of the troops. Rested they are and many too many for us. But there, that small shed. That's the target for this night's devilment."

Inyx surveyed the layout of the fort and the shed Nowless indicated. "Animals of some sort there?" she asked.

"Enough horses to let us ride with the very wind," said Nowless. "But while some of us try for the mounts, the rest of us will be doing what we can a'yonder."

"The mess hall?"

"What better place to spend a fine spring evening?"

Julinne glided up and handed Nowless a small vial of colorless liquid. He tapped the sides of the glass. Bubbles formed and rose to the top of the stoppered tube.

"You're going to poison them?" asked Ducasien, offended. "That's no way to fight a battle!"

"Aye, then, go and kill your twenty. No, make it forty since I have other things to be doing. While you're at it, lad, go on and slay all thousand of them because we're not able to."

"But the honor!" Ducasien protested. "This isn't an honorable form of battle. You kill your enemy with sword or dagger, not poison him like some foul cur."

"They're nothing more than animals to us. For all they've done to my people, I'd see them all tortured to death. This is as close as I can come," said Nowless. The man's tone had dropped from bantering to monotone. Inyx sensed how close he came to driving a dirk into Ducasien's ribs.

"Ducasien," she said urgently, "there are many ways of fighting. My experience along the Road has shown me that. There's nothing wrong with this."

"You forget yourself, Inyx," Ducasien said stiffly.

"These people fight for their very existence. The greys outnumber them because the grey-clads have been slaughtering them," she said, guessing accurately. "Haven't we seen the burned towns, the destroyed fields? What Claybore brings to this world is nothing less than genocide."

"It's not honorable," Ducasien said.

"Then don't fight," she said hotly. "But I will. Nowless needs all the help he can get. And I pledge my sword!"

"Well said, well said!" applauded Nowless. Ducasien eyed them in disgust, then reluctantly nodded that he, too, would join the disgraceful battle.

"But I will not use the poison," he added.

"Wouldn't think of it. That's my privilege." The sudden bitterness told Inyx that Nowless had lost much to Claybore's soldiers. He would gladly have used a knife on every one of the greys, had that been possible. This gave the best way of striking back.

"Let's be off." Nowless turned to Julinne and spoke quietly to the woman for several minutes, kissed her and went on down the hill. His bare feet made no sound on the ground as he walked. Inyx felt clumsy next to him.

At the gate Nowless signaled for them to wait. Two sentries marched slowly to and fro at their post. Before Inyx could decide how best to take out the one closest to her, the whistle of cast stones filled the air. Both guards crumpled to the ground like discarded foolscap. Almost without missing a step, two of Nowless's men picked up the sentry duties. In the dark their lack of uniforms wasn't obvious.

Inyx, Ducasien, Nowless, and three others slipped quietly into the compound.

"No disturbance to warn them, now," cautioned Nowless. They made their way directly for the mess hall. Nowless went inside while the others stood watch.

"I don't like this," mumbled Ducasien.

"It's all right," soothed Inyx. "Different worlds, different ways of waging war."

"I still prefer an honest sword fight."

"You," came the harsh voice. "Why are you loitering there? Don't you have other duties?"

"Please," spoke up Inyx. "We...well, we were just looking for a secluded spot."

The officer strode over. The instant he was within range, Inyx spun, drew her sword, and lunged. The tip of her blade caught the man directly in the groin. He grabbed his wounded crotch and let out a bleat liked kicked sheep. No other sound emerged from his mouth. Ducasien's strong hand clamped over his mouth. The other hand went to the back of the officer's head. One quick jerk broke the man's neck.

"Well met," complimented Nowless, emerging from the kitchens. "Dump him inside and let's be on our way."

"Wait!" Inyx shook her head. "If they find him inside they might do some checking. We can carry him with us. For a ways."

Nowless indicated that two of the men were to carry the slain officer. Inyx liked Nowless more and more. He was a brave man and a good leader not afraid to change plans when a better suggestion came up. She had seen men too stiff-necked to ever change their minds.

Like Lan Martak.

The thought of the brown-haired man, his gentle ways of loving, the times they had spent together before the magics so overwhelmed him brought a glistening to Inyx's blue eyes. She fought back the tears. How she wished he were here with her. But, like her long-dead husband, Lan was forever lost to her.

"Damn Claybore," she said viciously.

"Agreed," whispered Nowless, "but the thrice-damned mage has not been on this planet in long years. All we can do is remove the trash he left us."

The officer was unceremoniously dropped outside the gates to the fort. A signal brought the thunder of hooves as the rest of Nowless's band drove off the horses they weren't stealing.

Whether the sound alerted another guard or some other indiscretion had, alarm gongs sounded throughout the fort.

"We have a bit of a fight on our hands now," said Nowless. "We'd best let them get a ways down the road, don't you think?" He indicated those of his men escaping up the slopes.

"We can hold them long enough," said Inyx. "Ducasien has been longing for this, haven't you?"

"At last," the man cried, "an honorable way of fighting!"

Ten of Nowless's men rode up and held horses for them to mount, but by the time they'd settled into stirrup and saddle, the first wave of greys rushed from the fort.

Inyx's blade rose and dropped, severing an ear. She kicked another in the face and reined her mount around to face still another enemy. The woman's blade sang its restless song of death, and she was finally able to forget about Lan

Martak in the heat of the battle.

Only when they galloped off into the night, the cries of the grey-clad soldiers following them, did she again think of Lan.

There would have to be more slaughter—much more—for his memory to be erased totally.

CHAPTER FOUR

Krek lurched forward and settled into the crypt, long legs fitted tightly beneath his body. Leaving his friend Inyx troubled him, but staying with her troubled him even more. She would continually remind him of the good times they had spent with Lan Martak. Such a prod to the memory only produced morbid thoughts, Krek knew.

It was better to make a clean split, find a new world, walk new paths.

"I still will think of you, though," Krek said softly. He craned his mobile head around and peered out of the crypt to where Inyx and Ducasien stood side by side. The spider had no good feelings about Ducasien, but there were no bad ones, either. The man had come into Inyx's life at a time opportune for her. He would take care of her sorrows and comfort her, even if Krek were unable to find or give such solace.

The spells governing the cenotaphs began to churn and boil around him. The spider closed his dun-colored eyes and fell through space to a new world. Shades of grey forced themselves upon his mind and he had no sensation of tumbling, such as the humans often talked about experiencing.

Krek blinked and stirred in the closeness of the new crypt. Tensing strong legs, the spider lifted straight up. Strain as he might, the stone top refused to yield. Krek did not panic. He was a seasoned traveler along the Road and had often encountered similar predicaments on worlds seldom visited. Talons scraping at the stone sides of the crypt, Krek found a seam and worried at it until he enlarged it and broke off chunks of the crypt wall.

"Now," he said, with some feeling of accomplishment. In complete blackness, the arachnid dug and moved rock and dirt and forced his way out of the cenotaph and through an underground passage of his own devising. He disliked the closed-in feeling, preferring to swing freely on a web stretched between mountain peaks, but claustrophobia was alien to him. He remembered without any distaste the days spent within the cocoon, aware and yet unable to fight free. That was a memory of life as it was, another moment to be experienced and not dreaded.

But water?

Krek shuddered as he found the dirt turning increasingly wet. Soon enough, mud caked his furred legs. Krek tried to stop the involuntary trembling and failed. He dug faster, the dampness spurring him on. When he broke through the ground and saw the cloudy sky above he let out an anguished moan of stark despair.

"Noooo!" he sobbed. "This cannot be. It rains! I have come back to the world of burning water."

He used sharp mandibles to enlarge the opening onto this world and scrambled through, shaking himself as clean as he could. Tiny drops of rain pelted his hard carapace and trickled down his legs. The tingly sensation was not one he cherished. The idea of being wet all over thoroughly repelled him.

Krek ran for cover, shaking himself dry as he went. When he found a mausoleum door half open, he didn't hesitate pulling it wider and entering the dry, dusty interior.

An interesting web, he thought, looking at a pattern spun

by a tiny spider in one corner. Krek walked up the wall and hung upside down to peer at the geometry used. His head bobbed in agreement with the clever bindings, the assured use of the stone walls for foundations, the alternate sticky and clean pathways through the web itself. When a tiny fly inadvertently touched the center of the web, vibrations traveled from one side of the trap to the other.

"Ah, there you are," said Krek, chittering noisily. The minuscule spider in the web stopped on one strand, twisted around and stared at Krek, then let out tiny cries of indignation.

"He is your meal, not mine," Krek tried to reassure his distant cousin. "Why, he would make no more than an appetizer for me. Which reminds me of how long it has been since I have eaten. A disgrace. Imagine a celebrated Webmaster of the Egrii Mountains not eating in days and days. No succulent grubs or those pasty fungus plants Lan Martak was so fond of."

Krek fell silent as he thought about Lan Martak. He hardly noticed as the tiny spider hustled to the middle of the web and began spinning another web to encapsulate his prey. By the time the little spider had finished, a giant tear welled in Krek's left eye. It dripped dierctly down and onto the floor to form a tiny puddle. Curious ants deviated from their strict marching path to explore this phenomenon of water inside the mausoleum. They skirted the pond, delicately sampled it, and discarded any idea of its being useful. By the time Krek dropped from the ceiling, deftly twisting to land on his feet, the teardrop had vanished.

Not so his memories of Lan.

"How could you do this to me?" the giant spider asked over and over. "Oh, woe, woe! I am surely the most put upon of all creatures. Scorned by my only love, and rightly so, deserving no more than a craven's due, abandoned by my friends—no, not abandoned, *sent* away! I am so pitiful. So pitiful."

Krek peered out the door and saw that the light rain had vanished. Gingerly picking his path, he stepped from one dry spot to another until he came to a tall rock wall surrounding the cemetery grounds. He spat forth a short length of climbing web and went up the wall, perching on the narrow top and surveying this world he had blundered onto.

The shower had cleansed the air and left it crystal clear. From his vantage point Krek was able to see a considerable distance. And he liked what he saw.

Mountains, real *mountains,* rose up on the horizon.

"To build my web in some valley and simply dangle in the breeze," he said, venting a hefty sigh. "It would not be the same, not without Klawn, but the tranquility will do much to restore my good nature. Those days in the Egrii Mountains were so idyllic." He sighed again and continued to pivot about on the narrow wall.

Humans had built a largish town a few miles in the other direction, near a meandering stream. His sharp eyes picked out scores, hundreds, of the silly beings as they bustled about doing their confusing chores for all the most confusing of reasons. Krek saw nothing in the human village to attract him. If anything, he had had his fill of humans and their illogical ways.

"And some of them do not like spiders," he reminded himself. Krek had found a few worlds, before meeting Lan Martak, where the inhabitants actively hated spiders, a thing most ridiculous from his point of view. "They would certainly be better creatures if they would emulate their betters." Krek sniffed and kept turning.

To the far south he saw dust clouds rising. Squinting, the spider made out tiny dots he recognized as magically powered wagons. Lan Martak had tried to explain to him how a demon could be trapped in a boiler, heat water and make stream, and then use the steam to move wheeled vehicles. Krek held the opinion that humans wouldn't need such artificial devices if they only had the proper number of legs.

To the south, therefore, he saw nothing to hold his interest. Nor to the west did he see anything more than the humans' grain fields. A dreary occupation, that one. Krek

preferred the beauty and symmetry of a web and waiting
for his supper to come to him. Actually poking sticks in the
ground and hiding plant parts, tending them with more care
than they lavished on their own offspring, then cutting off
the plants after they had the temerity to actually grow confused Krek.

The mountains. To the north, he thought. A light jump
landed all eight feet solidly on the ground and headed him
in the direction of the distant range.

He quickly fell into the rolling gait that covered ground
steadily and, by the time he had walked twenty miles,
thoughts of Lan Martak and Inyx faded and anticipation for
what he'd find in the foothills grew.

Krek's mandibles clacked in futile rage at the sight of the
grey-clad legion marching through the hills. They had set
ablaze a human village and, even worse from the spider's
point of view, they had destroyed huge webs strung between
some of the deserted buildings on the village outskirts. Krek
had examined the webs with the hope of finding others of
his own size. The tiny spiders that populated this world did
not appear too communicative, but they showed no sign of
surprise or fear of him. He had hoped the old webs might
give a clue.

Now the webs were gone, set ablaze in the most foul
way. He had hidden some distance away and watched as
Claybore's soldiers doused the fragile webs with some vol-
atile liquid, then touched a spark to one corner. For a brief
instant, the entire web had been burning brightly, the strands
standing out in orange-and-white flames. Then the voracious
fire gulped down the web and went to work on the buildings.

Krek cared little about the humans. Let them do what
they would to one another. But he had a special fear and
loathing of the grey-clad ones. He saw what Lan Martak
meant when he said that they were different, had an evil
about them that transcended mere human foolishness. They
went out of their way to be mean.

The tongues of flame spread quickly and caused great

consternation among the villagers. The greys rounded them up and herded them off. And Krek watched it all.

Now he peered down from the majestic heights at the soldiers marching deeper into the hills to subjugate other villages. None stood for long against their armed and armored might. His mandibles ceased their spastic clacking and the spider relaxed. There had to be a spot so far away in the mountains that no human ever ventured to it. No humans, no grey-clad soldiers.

Krek walked up the side of a large boulder, over the top, and from there along a ridge and deeper into the mountains.

The rocks were so lovely, the spider reflected. They provided ample footholds and the surging peaks presented challenges in web design and construction techniques. Krek personally had spun no fewer than forty web patterns, one for each of the major uses and many decorative ones. It was only fitting, after all, for a Webmaster to be artistic as well as astute in all matters dealing with the web.

Krek lumbered along for almost a week and one sunny afternoon stopped to rest. He blinked at what lay revealed in a valley below him.

"Home!" he cried. Krek studied the web patterns and felt a twinge of nostalgia. While the geometries were subtly different, they looked enough like webs he and others had spun that they reminded him of his home in the Egrii Mountains. He bounced up and down on his long legs, hardly able to contain his joy.

"To feel the strands flying beneath the feet," he said with more zest than he'd felt in months. "To let the spinneret run free, the web flying out just so. Ah. . . ."

He hurried down the side of the mountain to the valley entrance. He canted his head to one side, listening. Krek heard nothing. His talons dug into the soft dirt and found bedrock. He felt for vibrations that might betray another's presence in the valley. Nothing. The spider wailed out his misery.

"All gone. They have left this fair valley. But why?"

Faint temblors reached his claws now. Krek turned and

looked in the direction of the disturbance. Caves led back into the mountainside. Why any spider would voluntarily seek out those holes when the webs were still intact, Krek didn't know. Some distant cousins of his preferred hiding in the ground, spinning their hunting webs over the doorways and trapping their prey in this fashion. It had always seemed a bit perverted to Krek, but still it was better than the odd ways the humans fed and sheltered themselves.

Krek was torn between the need to explore those caves for others of his kind and the mad desire to run along the aerial strands just once.

Desire overwhelmed him. He started up the sheer rock face of one cliff, saw the walking strand above him, jumped adroitly. His talons closed about the webstuff and held him firmly as his weight caused the elastic cable to stretch. He bounced, enjoying the feel once again. Then he hastened to the very center of the web.

There he gusted out one of his deep sighs and simply enjoyed life—the elevation, the feeling of dominance over the terrain, the way he came totally alive.

"Once more a Webmaster," he said aloud. The baleful howl of wind through the valley drowned out his words. Krek didn't care. This moment was too precious to waste. He swung back and forth, relishing the sensations he had been denied for so long.

Krek turned about in the web and looked down the length of the green valley. Tiny springs kept the vegetation lush and green but did not provide the odious ponds and splashing rivers he so hated. The constant hum of insects on which to feed told Krek this was nothing short of paradise. But where were the mountain arachnids? What forced them to abandon such a fine domain?

Krek ran lightly along one of the traveling strands and found an anchor point on the far wall of the canyon. He dug talons into the rock face and walked off the web and toward the caves he had seen. As he neared the yawning shaft, the telltale vibrations increased. Spiders. Many of them.

He paused at the mouth of the cave, then clacked and shittered and shrilled out a greeting of the proper form. Krek didn't expect an immediate reply. Such would be discourteous. Humans rushed everything so. One spoke, the other replied immediately. Spiders not only had the proper number of legs, they also knew how to conduct a polite conversation.

Twenty minutes later, a faint clacking echoed out of the cave.

Krek tried to figure out the dialect. The words jumbled and he had to puzzle out even that someone had responded to his polite inquiry about the valley.

"I am a Webmaster," he said. "May I pay homage to another?"

"He's dead," came the response so fast that Krek took a step back in surprise. Such unseemly haste in a spider showed intense agitation.

"These are not unusual occurrences," said Krek. "While I hope to enjoy a long life amid my hatchlings on the web runs, I, too, will die someday."

"They murdered him. *They set him on fire!*"

The anguish communicated perfectly to Krek. Nothing short of being soaked in water, and *then* set ablaze horrified him more. The coppery fur on his legs bristled, and he felt his body tensing to meet the challenge of anyone attempting to put the torch to him.

"The humans did it," came another, lighter voice. Krek recognized it as female. Not quite as lilting and lovely as that of his delightful Klawn, but still pleasant. "They drove us into the caves. We fear for our hatchlings."

"From the extent of your webs, there must be at least twenty of you," said Krek. He neglected to count hatchlings. Only adult arachnids were considered in populations since the younger spiders tended not to have long life-spans. The ones that weren't eaten often fell off the webs and died or met with other maiming misfortune.

"Only fourteen now." Krek mentally added about fifty hatchlings, of which five or ten might survive.

"Why do you hide in caves? This is not some new hunting technique, is it?"

"They might return at any moment. They are awful."

"The humans? Yes, they are all of that," agreed Krek. Then other pieces of this distressing picture came together for him. "These humans. Are they all dressed in a like manner? In uniforms?"

"You refer to the woven webs they hang around their frail bodies?" came the female's question.

"Yes. These are the most pernicious of the humans. A mage of great power and evil commands them."

"They do wear similar uniforms," she agreed.

Krek paused for the appropriate length of time, then asked, "Might I enter your cave?"

This time a polite delay elapsed before a simple, "Please do, Webmaster."

Krek ducked down and waddled into the cave. His eyes took several minutes to adjust to the dimness, then he pushed on ahead, careful not to touch any of the webs decorating the walls. He saw no one, nor had he expected to. The voices had echoed from a long ways into the cavern. Krek continued on until he came to a vast chamber.

He stood and studied the array of webbing, then clacked his mandibles together four times to indicate his approval.

"We are pleased by your acknowledgment of our pitiful efforts, Webmaster," said the small female spider.

Krek rubbed his front legs together in response while he looked her over. She was not bad looking—for a mere spider. Less than half Krek's eight-foot height and not even a quarter of his bulk, she still presented a trim, sprightly figure. Her spinnerets carried geometric decorations pleasing to the eye and her leg fur had been neatly tended. She reminded Krek a great deal of his long-lost love, Klawn— only this spider was so tiny, almost fragile.

"We have never seen one so large," spoke up another spider.

"For mere spiders, you have done well in spanning the vastness." Krek lifted a midleg and pointed to the intricate patterns displayed in the cavern. "Such fineness of strand, such daring spans, such beauty. I am impressed."

"Thank you, Webmaster," the female said.

"I am Krek-k'with-kritklik, Webmaster of the Egrii Mountains on a world far distant along the Cenotaph Road."

"I am Kadekk," said the female. Krek noted the lack of status claimed. He bobbed his head up and down in acknowledgment. It seemed reasonable. She was only a mere spider and hardly in the same class as his Klawn.

"We are in exile in this cave," moaned one of the other spiders. "Our Webmaster died a foul death at the hands of the silly humans."

"The soldiers," said Krek, "are the worst of the humans. A mage guides their hand in their hideous deeds." He shivered lightly at the thought of being drenched, dried, and set afire. It was something Claybore's troops would consider good sport. His mandibles ground together as he unconsciously wished for their commanders' heads between the serrated jaws.

Kadekk said, "We need leadership and you are so... much a Webmaster."

The way Kadekk asked made Krek puff up with pride. He had always known of his own nobility, and it pleased him these mere spiders recognized it immediately.

"Would you be our Webmaster and help fight these humans?"

"It is nothing I have not done before," Krek said. But in the back of his mind rose the troubling thought, *But always before Lan Martak has been with me.*

"Another legion moves up the valley," said one of the smallest of the spiders, hardly more than a hatchling. "We will be burned out of even this cave unless we stop them."

"Since I did not pass them on my way into the valley, this means they come from the far end," said Krek.

"There is a large ground web of them two human days' travel away. They find our fine valley necessary for their depredations on the other humans."

"They have bases or forts," said Krek, thinking. "Not ground webs. They are not sufficiently advanced for that." He settled down and pulled in his long legs. In this position he was on a level with the mere spiders. His agile mind worked over various plans, then he decided. "We go immediately. Unseemly haste is required for survival."

Fifteen of the mere spiders followed Krek. He was irrationally happy to see that Kadekk joined them and stayed close by his side.

"All is ready, Webmaster Krek." Kadekk bounced around from one strand to the next, her nimble feet skipping over the sticky cables and finding only the walking strands.

"Just in time," said Krek. He indicated the dusty path of the soldiers.

The grey-clads trooped along, one hundred strong. In their hands they carried the worst weapons of all—torches. As it was midday, these were intended for firing webs, not lighting a dark path.

"Now, Webmaster, do we attack now?" came the anxious chittering from along the valley.

"Not yet," Krek answered. "But soon. Very soon." He thought back to the other battles he had fought, the cowardice he had shown—and the courage. It seemed that Lan Martak's presence, and even friend Inyx's, helped him live up to his duties as Webmaster. Without them, his courage sometimes flagged and he did weak things. Now he fought without them, but the reasons were noble. Krek could not in good faith allow these pathetic little mere spiders to perish simply because their Webmaster had been so foully murdered.

"... the buggers now," came the faint words drifting up from the valley floor. "Set your torches." Hearty laughter echoed the length and breadth of the valley as the troops lit their torches and prepared to burn out the webs and their spiders.

"Krek, they ... they will burn us!" Kadekk shrilled.

"Drop webs at either end of the valley," Krek ordered. He rubbed his legs together in satisfaction when he saw the immense hunting webs lowered to block escape. Only when he was sure all the grey-clads had their torches ignited did Krek give the next order.

"Drop the climbing webs."

From both sides of the canyon soared the powdery, dry climbing webs. In feathery clouds they flew out and floated downward, the air retarding descent of the light, strong webs.

"But Krek, the torches will burn them," protested Kadekk.

"I do not have time to explain," Krek said. "Watch and learn how to use their ghastly fire weapons against them. I really do not know if even such as they deserve this fate." Krek thought on it for a moment before adding, "Yes, they do. They do deserve all they will get."

The first layer of dry web reached a halfway point. Krek gave the signal for another toss to send even more webbing out. By the time he ordered the third flight of webstuff, the first had reached the ground. The soldiers held their torches aloft, laughing and making crude comments. The laughter turned to shrieks of fear as the web caught fire and continued to fall around them, sending twenty-foot-high tongues of fire into the sky.

"They burn themselves in our webs!" cried Kadekk.

"Their weapon has been used against them. Keep sending down more dry web." Krek watched with bloodthirsty satisfaction as the troops tried in vain to extinguish their torches. But for them it was too late. The webs had been fired and now descended, clouds of flaming death dropping and clinging to their clothing. Dozens of grey-clads were set ablaze and ran shrieking as they incinerated.

"Krek, the others. Some escaped." Kadekk pointed out almost a score of soldiers who had evaded the burning webs.

"Now *we* fight," said Krek. He spat out a long climbing strand and anchored it to the side of the cliff. The arachnid kicked free and lowered himself to the floor of the valley. He amazed himself with the bravery he showed in the face of so much fire burning away merrily as it consumed underbrush and human soldier with equal hunger.

Kadekk dropped beside him. Together they and five other spiders lumbered off in pursuit. By the time they overtook the frightened, fleeing soldiers, six had already become tangled in the hunting web blocking the mouth of the valley. The others spun, drew weapons, and faced the wave of spiders.

Krek's presence turned the tide. None of the grey-clads had seen a spider this large, and their moment of panic allowed him to slice four in half before the others responded. Seeing their feared enemies felled with single slashes of Krek's mighty mandibles, the mere spiders fell to the fight with new courage and determination.

Blood soaked into the dusty floor of the canyon. All the soldiers and three of the mere spiders perished.

"What of the ones in the hunting web?" asked Kadekk, eyeing the captives. "We can kill them with no effort."

"Spare them," ordered Krek.

Those hung in the web relaxed visibly. They were to be spared.

"Cocoon them and save them as dinner for our hatchlings. They are tasty enough, even if they do not have the proper number of legs."

The human shrieks soon stopped when the cocooning webs enfolded their struggling bodies. Krek and Kadekk climbed back to the heights to plan new webs for the valley.

It felt good being Webmaster once more.

CHAPTER FIVE

"Noooooo!" Lan Martak screamed as he whirled through nothingness. The world of summer scents and brightly blooming flowers and airy breezes vanished when Claybore's spell took hold. Lan reached out magically and clung to Kiska k'Adesina, keeping her beside him. If he had to spend an eternity lost in the whiteness between worlds, he would not spend it alone.

"Oh, yes, Martak," came the scornful words. Claybore enjoyed his revenge to the hilt. "You now find yourself lost. Remember how it was when I did this to that bitch Inyx? You sought her out and only succeeded in bringing her back because of the help you had. This time there is no aid for you. None. You are lost!"

The laughter following faded away until only deathly silence remained behind.

Lan walked through the cloaking whiteness, aware of Kiska nearby but not seeing her. The weight of responsibility for her drove him to seek her out. The task proved more difficult than he'd imagined. Even though Lan had successfully found the disembodied Inyx in this place between

worlds when Claybore had exiled her here, he had forgotten
how truly alien the white nothingness was.

Time ceased to have meaning. He walked and he thought
of all that had happened. The magical battle had been pre-
mature on his part, yet he hadn't been totally unprepared.
Meeting with the Resident of the Pit had definitely alerted
Claybore to his presence on that world, even if the small
magic used in battle with the grey-clad soldiers hadn't. But
the sight of the Pillar of Night again stunned Lan and allowed
Claybore to work his spells unhindered.

Why? What was it about the black column that devoured
all light that so paralyzed him? He was not afraid of it or
the magics locked within it, yet he knew he ought to be.
There came from it an undeniable power, and the Resident
was unable to tell him of it. In some fashion the magics
robbed the Resident of godhood and reduced a once mighty
deity to little more than a wishing well.

But what a wishing well! Lan guessed that there were
pits on every world along the Road. His mind turned to
other avenues of attack. If the Resident of the Pit existed
simultaneously on each world, might it not be possible to
walk the Road using those pits? Where was the magic for
that? Lan searched for the proper chant, the incantation that
would reveal any such well in this whiteness, and failed.

He turned—or not, since it hardly mattered—and saw
Kiska k'Adesina. She had become a ghostlike figure, transparent and flickering in and out of sight like a guttering
candle flame. Lan lost her as gauzy curtains floated between
them, then found her, much to his disgust, by using the
geas Claybore had laid upon him. His *love* for her drew
them together.

"Lan," gasped Kiska as she grabbed for his arm. "I never
thought I'd be happy to see you. What is this place?"

Lan Martak didn't answer.. The geas forced him to joy
on being reunited with Kiska, but he knew there was no
true love. For Inyx he would have stranded himself in this
nothing place if she could only have walked free on some
world of substance. But for Kiska, he would not trade spit
for her company, given free will.

But an idea began forming. His spells were useless, that he knew. Could Claybore's geas provide the thread leading out of this white desolation? Lan smiled wryly at that. To use Claybore's own spell to unlock a more deadly one amused him. It almost vindicated his claim to being a mage.

Try as he would, though, all Lan succeeded in finding was a hint as to the direction, a glimmering of hope that he had enough power held in reserve to accomplish the task.

"Lan?" Kiska moved closer and yet the distance between them did not change. "I feel as if I am coming apart. Drifting apart inside. Everything is so . . . dreamy."

"The space between worlds does not follow ordinary laws. My spells fail and force is useless." He lightly touched the hilt of his sword. Creatures roamed through the whiteness, but they fought in ways he had never mastered. If magic and blade availed him nothing, how did he defend himself? He renewed his efforts to follow the trail back to Claybore's world.

"I don't like it here. I want to go somewhere else. Lan, take me away from this."

Power surged inside Lan. The geas to love Kiska, to keep her from harm and to please her, added to his ability. The thready indications of magic he spied became clearer, dark dots occasionally hidden by the movements of the white landscape. Lan followed the trail as he would any spoor in the forest.

"Who?" came the distant question.

Lan tried to ask Kiska what she meant, but the woman was again separated from him, more by mind than distance. Even though she clung to his arm, they were poles away from one another—and someone else again asked, "Who is there?"

"We are lost between worlds. Claybore's spell holds us here. Can you help?"

"Where?"

"Here," Lan said. He formed a mental image of the whiteness and sent it out, as he would a spell. The thready path they followed became more distinct.

"I see you and yet I do not. This is perplexing."

"Help us."

For a long while no answer came. Lan feared he had made contact with another mage—one in Claybore's camp. He had not forgotten how the mage Patriccan had given him such problems when Claybore had laid seige to Iron Tongue's walled city. Lan thrust the metal tongue in his mouth out and lightly touched the very tip. It heated, indicating spells about him of which he knew nothing. The legacy of Claybore's tongue had brought him both augmented magical powers and woe. For all the newfound ability it gave him, it also took its toll on his humanity.

"Help me," he said, using the Voice. The tongue warmed even more. The potent spell rippled along the black band leading off into the whiteness.

"Do not think me such a fool," came the instant warning. "I am no novice."

"Help me, please," Lan said, toning down his command and making it a plea. "Without your aid we will be lost here. Show me the way back."

"Very well."

The black thread widened. Lan coaxed it and the mage on the other end spread it out until it stood as wide as a footpath through the forest. Lan and Kiska hurriedly followed it.

"Lan!" shrieked Kiska, when they had walked for what seemed hours. Her sword slid free of its sheath and cut through white nothingness to one side of the path. "Did you see it?"

A hulking creature loomed up once more. Its skin had faded to glasslike transparency and revealed the sturdy skeletal structure within. The only parts of the beast that seemed the least bit solid were the six-inch-long fangs in the vicious mouth. Lan tried a fire spell, only to have it snuffed out inches from his hand. He drew his sword and slashed downward. He caught the creature high on one shoulder and tried to cleave it open to the groin.

His blade bit into a clavicle, then found only mist.

"You wounded it, Lan. It...it attacks!" Kiska's voice

betrayed fear but her actions were those of a soldier. She did not even consider retreat. She widened her stance and prepared to meet the brutal assault head on.

The creature spun from Lan's punishing blade at the last instant and ducked under Kiska's sword. She thrust high and missed. Fangs sank into her thigh.

Kiska moaned and tried to cut the beast's back. Her sword found only mist. Lan drove it back and into the whiteness.

"What is happening? I sense disturbance," came the other mage's words.

"We were attacked. If we don't win free soon, we might never make it." He looked anxiously at Kiska's wound. It bled, but not in the fashion of most bites. The blood came out in perfect, expanding circles, like the ripples on a small pond when a rock is dropped into the water. Lan tried to staunch the flow from the curious wound but only made it worse.

"Follow my familiar," the other mage commanded.

But Lan saw nothing. He helped Kiska along the black pathway, not knowing where it led. The tiny hints he received about their rescuer only raised more questions than they answered. In some fashion he sensed the other mage was also bound to Claybore, but not as he was through the geas linking him inexorably to Kiska k'Adesina.

"There!"

Lan lifted his gaze to see what excited Kiska. It hardly seemed possible. An archway of solid stone stood in the midst of the whiteness. Through the arch he saw a well-appointed room. A figure sat in a high-backed carved wood chair, obscured by shadows.

"Through the door," he said, one arm around Kiska. He rushed forward, but again distances proved different in the white mists. Hours, years, centuries passed before he stepped through the archway and into the solid room.

"Oh," he said, dropping to his knees. Kiska's weight almost proved more than he could bear. He eased her to the floor. The wound on her thigh now flowed bright red in a way that meant an artery had been severed.

"She needs healing," said the other mage.

"I can do it, I think," said Lan. "The spells are not overly complex."

"Show me."

He nodded. He started the spell without recourse to the magics locked within his tongue. When he was sure the watching mage had learned what he did, Lan used the Voice.

"Heal!" he commanded, building the potent healing spell and driving it through Kiska's flesh and to the severed artery.

"She is pale but the artery is mended," said the other.

"Good." Lan wiped sweat off his forehead and tried to get a good look at his benefactor. Instead, he saw a looking glass on the wall across the room reflecting the image of the archway.

Lan Martak spun, hand going to sword. He whipped out the blade and lunged just as the seven-foot-long beast emerged fully from the space between worlds. The six-inch fangs dripped red—Kiska's blood. But all that saved them from death was the spurting wound on the shoulder that Lan had given the creature in the whiteness. It lurched to one side and its spring was aborted.

Lan's lunge went true, piercing the creamy furred chest. The beast let out an ear-shattering bellow of pain and jerked away. Lan's sword was pulled from his hand.

He reached for his dagger, then remembered they were no longer between worlds. If they had returned to Claybore's planet, then Lan's arsenal of magical weapons worked. He straightened and faced the slavering monster. Yellowed teeth were exposed as lips pulled back. Talons lashed at the air in front of the creature as it gathered powerful hindquarters under it for the killing leap.

A fireball exploded from Lan's fingertips. A loud sizzling filled the room as the greenish fire touched fur and flesh and began burning. Only when the beast's heart had been turned into a cinder did the magical fire dwindle and finally extinguish.

"Whew," Lan said. "Being in the mists must have addled

my brain. My spells didn't work there and I had to use my sword. Facing this again, it never occurred to me that a spell would defeat it so quickly."

"Your swordplay was expert," came a light, musical voice. "Your magics even more so."

Lan turned to see the other mage for the first time. He had been groggy due to passing from nothingness to a real world. Now he was simply speechless from admiration. The mage rescuing him was not only a woman, she was a stunningly gorgeous woman. Long cascades of white-blonde hair fell past her shoulders. Grey eyes probed questioningly into his very soul and found answers. Lush, full red lips curled into a pleasant smile, one that Lan wanted to enjoy.

Her figure was even more captivating than her smile. Purple velvet cloaked her body, clinging to her with static intensity. She brushed back a vagrant strand of hair falling into her eyes and turned slightly, perching on the edge of a carved wood table.

"You seem startled. Do you recognize me?" she asked.

"Never could I forget you, had we met." Lan introduced himself.

"I am Brinke."

Lan bowed deeply. Brinke smiled at his attempt at the courtly gesture.

"You are not used to such things, are you?" she asked. "You seem so unlike mere courtiers."

"I'm not," Lan admitted. He cursed his rough upbringing. How he wished for the polish of a court dandy now.

"Yet you control magics of incredible power and versatility." A note came into Brinke's voice that alerted Lan to hidden dangers. "You neglected to mention your friend." Brinke pointed to where Kiska lay unconscious.

"No friend mine," Lan said bitterly. "She is one of Claybore's personal staff, a commander high in his esteem." The words choked him now; he felt the full force of the geas strangling him. "I . . . I love her," he grated out between clenched lips.

"So?" Brinke moved around the table and sat in her chair.

She tented slender, gold-ringed fingers and peered at him over the top. Lan flinched under the intensity of the grey eyes, yet no spell was uttered. What magics Brinke used were only natural ones.

"I can't help myself," Lan said, fighting to keep control. "Claybore placed me under a geas. I...I can't counter it. She is a dagger against my throat. Claybore cares nothing for her except as an instrument of my destruction."

"She has tried to kill you several times." Brinke's words came as a simple statement, not a question. Lan nodded. "He saves her for the ultimate confrontation, then. If he succeeds in killing you without using her, however he intends to do that, fine. Otherwise, he always has a spy and ally in your camp." Brinke shook her head, white-blonde hair fluttering up in disarray.

Lan glanced over to the mountain of dead carcass and asked, "Is there some way of removing that? I have no wish to keep it as a trophy."

"Ugly, isn't it? I've never seen its like around here."

"There's no way to find out what world it came from. The space between worlds contains beings from all, I think."

Brinke made a small gesture. From a tiny closet set off to one side of the room came small demon-powered cylinders, rolling on rubber wheels. They hissed and complained but taloned arms came forth and grabbed at the carcass. The fronts of the cylinders opened and the demons began sucking in noisily until the beast vanished. Only then did the cleaners belch, whirl about, and return to their stations in the closet.

"You must tell me more of this," Brinke said, pointing at Kiska. "Would you like me to kill her for you?"

Lan's reaction came instinctively. Brinke slammed back in her chair as the spell sought to crush the life from her body. Only through extreme exertion did Lan lighten the spell he cast and then destroy it totally.

"I'm sorry," he mumbled.

"This geas is more than I had thought," the woman said softly. "But it could not be a common spell or a mage of your ability would have lifted it himself." Brinke rose and said, "We'll see that she's put to bed. While your healing spells seemed adequate, let's have the chirurgeon examine her."

Lan picked Kiska up in his arms and followed Brinke through a maze of corridors. Glimpses out narrow windows showed the full bloom of summer on the land; he had returned to the world where the Pillar of Night beckoned so seductively to him.

"Claybore is not likely to know of your rescue," Brinke said as she ushered Lan into a sleeping chamber. She indicated he ought to put Kiska on the bed. He lowered her gently, even as he wanted to throw her from the high window. "This castle is shielded against his intrusions."

"You bear some burden put upon you by Claybore. What is it?"

She swallowed, then pulled herself up stiff-necked, eyes staring at a blank wall.

"I don't know," she said. "I know he has placed a geas on me, also, but its nature is hidden from me. I fear it." She turned and gripped Lan's brawny forearm. "Oh, how I fear not knowing what he might make me do. The uncertainty is worse than any deed he might make me perform."

Lan snorted at that. "Claybore's imagination is vivid. You might be better off not knowing." But he understood the woman's concern. Only because he had advanced to a stage almost matching Claybore's had he been able to detect the geas forcing him to protect Kiska. Lan needed to surpass Claybore in ability to be able to counter the spell. He wondered if the answer lay locked within the beguiling Pillar of Night.

"Lan?" called out Kiska. "What happened?"

"Rest," he said. "I'll be here. There's someone coming to examine you, to make sure your injuries aren't worse than I thought."

Brown eyes moved past Lan to fix on Brinke. Lan saw the calculation working in Kiska's expression. He made no move to introduce the two.

"She is very lovely," said Kiska.

"I will fetch the chirurgeon," said Brinke, moving from the room with a liquid grace that reminded Lan of Inyx stalking game.

"She likes you. I can tell," said Kiska.

"I used a small healing spell on your leg wound. All that saved you was the odd flow of time between worlds. An artery had been severed by the beast's fanging. Only when we emerged back onto this world did the wound begin to bleed."

"The Pillar of Night is near?" Kiska asked. "Never mind. It must be. I recognize this world. It was here that Claybore and I—" Kiska abruptly cut off her words and smiled wickedly. "That is no concern of yours, dear, loving Lan." The words burned as if they had been dipped in acid.

Brinke returned with the chirurgeon, who performed a thorough and nonmagical examination. All the while Lan and Brinke stood to one side, quietly talking.

When the chirurgeon left, Lan said, "I should stay with her."

"No, darling Lan," spoke up Kiska. "I would rest. He gave me a sleeping potion. I . . . grow drowsy. Go and swap spells with her." A tiny smile curled the corners of Kiska's mouth. Lan couldn't help but compare the difference between the two women. On Brinke a smile brought sunshine; on Kiska it chilled to the bone. "Go and leave me alone. I would sleep now." Kiska pulled a blanket over her shoulder and turned her head away.

Lan and Brinke silently left the room and made their way back to Brinke's study. Another of the magically powered cleaning devices scuttled about to clean the beast's blood from the flagstone floor. Lan went and stood in front of the archway.

"It doesn't appear to lead anywhere now," he said. "What spells do you use to activate it?"

"My magics are not so predictable," Brinke said. "I know few spells. I sit and sometimes everything *seems* right. Then I perform what strike me as miracles; but, on a consistent basis, I have no control."

"You plucked me from the nothingness," said Lan.

"I sat here reading and a mood came over me. I felt . . . apprehensive. I spoke, you answered. If I used some spell or another, I know nothing of it."

"Purely instinctual," Lan mused.

"I have made no real effort to learn formally."

Lan's heart accelerated as he looked at Brinke. Her beauty was unmatched on any of the worlds he had walked. He told her so.

"What will Claybore's militant pawn think of such flowery words?" Brinke asked.

"I don't know."

A sinking feeling gripped Lan Martak. Kiska had almost chased him away, knowing full well what it would lead to. Why? What part did this have in Claybore's plot? Any?

His and Brinke's eyes locked. He moved closer to her.

"I should thank you for all you've done."

"No thanks is necessary," Brinke said. Her tongue slipped the merest fraction from her mouth, wetting her lips. Lan kissed her.

The kiss became more, much more. Through the long, passionate night, Lan never once thought of Kiska.

But he did think of lost Inyx.

CHAPTER SIX

"Tell me all you see," Ducasien said earnestly. He bent forward, his arm around Inyx. "There must be details you can ferret out with this wondrous talent of yours, Julinne. Show me. Show *us*."

"It," said Nowless, "does not work that way with her. Not always. Julinne's wondrous fair talent is limited, even at the best of times. What hellish horrors she has been through makes it all the more difficult for her."

"Julinne," said Inyx, reaching out and holding one of the woman's hands in both of hers, "this is a turning point in history. With your vision of the grey-clads' base we can eliminate them. We can drive them from this world once and for all time."

Julinne nodded, a bleak expression on her face. "I am unable to choose between my sight and the *seeing*."

"Try," urged Inyx. "For all those you've lost to those accursed butchers, try."

Julinne turned a shade whiter; it made her look less healthy than many corpses Inyx had seen along the Road. Julinne had lost four children and a husband to Claybore's troops

67

and along with the heartbreak came a boon. The shock of
the loss had broken the woman's spirit and, ironically, had
given her the gift required to defeat the grey-clads.

"How many?" asked Ducasien, his voice low and sooth-
ing.

Julinne's eyes glazed over. "Four hundred and some."

"When will they all be together? When will the commandant muster his troops?" Ducasien and Inyx exchanged
worried looks. Julinne turned even paler and her entire body
trembled like a leaf in a high wind. Even her teeth chattered
in reaction.

"A fortnight from now. They gather to . . . to . . ."

"Yes?" Inyx held the woman's hand and squeezed re-
assuringly. "What is their plan?"

"I see it so clearly," Julinne said. "But the words. The
words refuse to come."

"This is harmful to her," protested Nowless. "We cannot
go on."

"We must!" snapped Ducasien. "I tell you this is the only
chance we will have to destroy them. gather them in one
spot and close the trap around them." He clapped his hands
together. Jaw set and face grim, Ducasien brooked no argument.

"So many of us have died," moaned Julinne.

"More will unless you tell us the plan." Inyx listened
carefully as Julinne's lips barely moved. The whispered
words began to make sense and she passed them along to
Ducasien and Nowless. When the woman's vision of the
future had come to an end, she slumped forward. Inyx
caught her and gently laid her down. Julinne slept deeply.

Ducasien motioned for them to leave the woman. He,
Inyx, and Nowless walked the perimeter of the guerrilla
camp, discussing all Julinne had seen.

"They feel they have committed enough outrage," said
Ducasien. "The time is ripe for them to systematically eliminate us."

"The countryside is properly dispirited," admitted Nowless. "Even our finest victories do little to help when the

farmers know that the bedamned grey-clads might descend on them at any time and burn them out."

"They have no confidence in us," said Inyx. "But we need that. Without full support by the time the soldiers gather at the fort, we are lost."

"You have a plan?" asked Ducasien.

Inyx nodded, brushing away her long, dark hair. Her blue eyes sparkled as she launched into it.

"A resounding defeat for a small group of them will set us up nicely," she said. "We show the countryside we can prevail. That will align them with us. But the victory cannot be so great that it alerts the greys."

"You're thinking thoughts of Marktown?" asked Nowless. "The garrison there is undermanned, yet it is a key position for them."

"It will be our most dangerous raid yet," said Inyx, "but if we succeed, we will have won."

"Not quite," said Ducasien. "Their mage will have returned from his circuit. The fort will boast both soldiers and ward spells. The mage is not overly good, but he is better than none at all, which is what we have." Ducasien clasped his hands behind his back and walked on. Nowless said nothing as he turned and left.

Inyx watched Ducasien, thinking that they ought to have a mage.

"Lan," she said softly, then hastened after Ducasien.

"We are too few," complained Ducasien. "This raid cannot work as you laid it out. We must regroup, plan some other foray."

Inyx laughed. "You are too caught up in the overall scheme to appreciate the subtle moves. Look, Ducasien, we go yonder and down. The greys rush out to meet us. Nowless and his group sneak in from behind and we have them caught in a pincer. They cannot run and we will outfight them because they are undermanned."

"Too pat," said Ducasien. The man chewed on his lower lip and looked worried.

"There is something more bothering you. This is not that daring a plan."

"You," Ducasien said finally. "I do not want you in the party. Stay with Julinne and the others."

"Why this sudden change of heart?" Inyx frowned. This was unlike Ducasien.

"I . . . I have lost too much," said Ducasien. "I will not lose you."

"Oh? And you think I have not lost those I love?" she shot back. "My husband is worm food because of the grey-clads. What if I should lose you to their sword? Would my hurt be less than yours?"

"This is a foolish argument."

"It is," Inyx said hotly. "I plan, I fight. I must show confidence in my skills or none will follow."

Ducasien faced Marktown and the small garrison. He kept his hands locked behind his back, a gesture Inyx had long since interpreted as being one of defiance in the man. But she would not relent. Inyx knew she was right in all she did.

"Leponto province was never like this, was it?" he asked.

"Not in your memory," Inyx said. "I left just as the soldiers poured over the borders from Jux and Chelanorra. For years they had been threatening such a move, but it was only when Reinhardt and his brothers were dead did they invade us."

"That was long years before I was even born," said Ducasien. "The time flows between worlds in odd ways."

"Tell me of Leponto. The one you remember." Inyx leaned back against the sun-warmed rock and closed her eyes. No longer stretched out at her feet was the village of Marktown on some world so far along the Road she had no clear idea where it lay. Ducasien's words took her home, where she had been born and raised and loved and watched death stalk those dearest to her. Back to Leponto.

"The summer I left was extraordinary," Ducasien said. "The *lin* were in full bloom. Remember how the blossoms showed brown spirals?"

"Only in the blue blooms," said Inyx, remembering well. "The red blooms had black spirals. When I was a child we'd pretend we were bugs going along the spiral. We'd describe our path to one another."

"Pollen grains," said Ducasien. "We'd always try to be the first to describe the pollen. As large as boulders."

"You played the game, too? Yes, I suppose all in our province would. The flowers were the mainstay of life."

Inyx sighed. Leponto had been famed throughout the world for the delicacy of its flowers, especially the *lin*. Some had curative powers, others were used in dyes. Nowhere in the world had a finer textile factory than in Leponto. And the flowers even had decorative value. The Council of Threes always opened with a flower from Leponto being presented to each of the representatives. Inyx had traveled to the court once for the ceremony. Seeing the three from her home given the *lin* had been a high point of her young life.

"The autumn feast," went on Ducasien. He chuckled. "I met my first lover at the feast."

"Under the moons of good harvest?" asked Inyx, startled. "So did I."

"Reinhardt?"

Inyx smiled and shook her head. "Reinhardt was later, but not that much so. No, I had forgotten about the autumn feast until you'd mentioned it."

"You're lying," chided Ducasien. "No one forgets their first lover. Their second, perhaps, or their fourth or fortieth, but never their first."

Inyx swallowed and nodded assent. She had not forgotten. She had remembered how much he looked like Lan Martak. The brown hair and eyes, the quick movements, the quicker smile. They had met under the watchful eyes of the orange harvest moons. Inyx lifted one finger to a spot just under her left eye; he had kissed her there. The finger traced a line down to the line of her jaw and then forward to her chin. His lips had moved along so enticingly. Even now Inyx felt her heart beating faster. Her hand covered her lips.

"It's time to assemble our troops," said Inyx. "We dare not put this off any longer."

"The patrols will not return until sundown," said Ducasien.

"We attack now."

Ducasien locked his hands behind his back and his lips thinned to a razor's slash, but he did not argue. He went to give Nowless and the others last-minute instructions. Inyx gazed downhill and saw Leponto in autumn. She closed her eyes and when she looked again saw only Marktown.

It was time to begin the attack.

Inyx fingered her sword and worried. Something was wrong. She glanced around and noted the placement of her fighters. All waited nervously for the signal to attack Marktown garrison. The woman licked dried lips and forced calm on herself. She had to think. What wasn't right? What was out of place?

"Nowless and the others are ready," said Ducasien. He dismissed the messenger, who trotted back to the ranks and waited for further orders. "Let's get this done."

"No," said Inyx.

"We can't retreat. You said so yourself. We must go forward."

"Something's not right. How I wish Lan were here. He'd know." Inyx agonized over her feelings. She had learned to trust them and they told her disaster awaited any frontal assault. But why?

"We go." Ducasien's face darkened. Inyx knew the mention of Lan Martak triggered the rage and pulled a curtain of emotion over his good sense.

"With caution," she said.

"In battle? Don't be absurd. We go, we fight, we win! To Marktown!" he cried, lifting his sword high in the air. Sunlight glinted off the blued steel blade and signaled the fighters on either side. With a ragged cheer, they began moving, slowly at first and then with increased momentum as they ran downhill.

Inyx sucked in a deep breath and followed. She would not be left behind. If this were a trap laid by the grey-clads, she wanted to be beside Ducasien when it closed around them. She had lost too many who were dear to her.

"See?" panted Ducasien as they reached the outskirts of the village. "All goes as we planned."

Inyx agreed it was true. The garrison of soldiers had been caught unawares. The gates were still open and most of them lounged about outside their tiny fort. The front of the assault wave hit and engaged the soldiers, many of whom didn't even have weapons. It was slaughter—and Inyx forgot her misgivings and joined in.

The main body of greys rushed from the garrison, armed and ready for combat. By this time she saw Nowless and his select few skulking at the edges. When the soldiers rushed forth, Nowless slipped into the garrison proper. When the pitiful few survivors returned—if any did—they would find themselves trapped with a fresh, savage fighting team.

Inyx met a doublehanded sword slash with a parry that made her sword ring like a bell. Her opponent was taller and much stronger. His biceps strained the seams of his grey uniform and his collar hung open because his thick neck had tensed and ripped off the fastener.

"Filth," he grunted as he swung again. Inyx danced away, knowing she couldn't continue matching this man's strength. The blade cut air a fraction of an inch in front of her face. "You killed Droy. He was my best friend."

A circular cut missed by a larger margin, but Inyx knew she could not hope to wear this one down. His great stamina would be enhanced by fighting rage and need to revenge his fallen comrade. Inyx almost felt sorry for him as she judged the range, waited for another berserk cut to miss and then launched a long, precise lunge. The tip of her blade spitted him in the side.

She danced back as the man stupidly looked at the blood gushing from between his ribs.

"Slut. You won't kill me. You won't!" With a bull-throated roar, he lowered his sword and charged. Inyx felt as if she'd dislocated her shoulder as she parried his blade and then lunged as hard as she could. Her blade slid past the man's belly, opening it in a giant bloody gash. The grey took three more steps, straightened, and tried to hold his guts inside and failed. He toppled like a felled tree.

"Good work," said Ducasien, sliding to a halt beside the woman. "I couldn't get free." Love shone in his eyes. "You are unique. Of all the women I have known, none matches you."

Inyx caught her breath and stared at the grey on the ground. "We'd killed his best friend. All he fought for was revenge."

"We wouldn't have killed his friend if the grey-clads hadn't tried to subjugate this entire world."

"They're only pawns. They fight because they can do nothing else. Claybore uses them and tosses them away when they outgrow their mission."

"Stop them, stop Claybore."

"I think Lan was right. Stop Claybore, stop them. Without the head to direct the arm, they wouldn't fight. And he wouldn't lose his best friend in a guerrilla raid."

Ducasien didn't share her concern. "They're better off dead, then, than being puppets for Claybore."

Inyx didn't reply. A stirring deep within caused her to stare at the open gates of the garrison. Her plan had worked perfectly. When the soldiers had seen they couldn't outfight the guerrillas, they had retreated to the supposed safety of their fort. Nowless and his men cut them down as they entered.

If she wanted to, Inyx could claim the garrison. But that wasn't part of the plan. Patrols of considerable strength still roamed the countryside. This foray had been intended only to show a dagger aimed at the heart, not the actual thrust to the death.

"Nowless," she called out, waving to get the man's attention. "Did you find anything inside the garrison?"

"Only dead greys." Nowless laughed and held aloft his bloody sword and dagger.

"There is more," she said. "I feel it. Being with Lan has taught me to sense magic. Not understand it, but sense it."

"Stop it!" demanded Ducasien. "Stop talking about Martak. He left you. He refused to rescue you when he had the chance. Stop talking about him."

"We are in danger, Ducasien. Signal the retreat. Do it now!"

"You're overwrought," he said. "We want to burn down the garrison and show the people we have the strength to..." His words trailed off. In the distance a pillar of dust rose. Ducasien frowned and said, "There's no wind today. What causes that?"

"Magic. Call the retreat."

Even as Inyx spoke, the other fighters gathered around and stared at the dancing, billowing brown column. They spoke quietly among themselves, commenting on the oddity. It moved toward Marktown with a speed that belied any natural phenomenon.

"Back to the hills," shouted Inyx. The fighters stood rooted to the spot, watching. A sense of dread built inside Inyx. Magics!

The dust cloud died down and a young man dismounted from a horse. But Inyx saw that the horse's hooves did not touch ground. The steed floated the barest fraction of an inch above. The young man patted his animal on the neck and pulled his cloak around his shoulders as if he were unconcerned about the men who had just killed an entire garrison of soldiers.

He strutted over and eyed them with disdain. "A ragtag crew. Hardly a good opposition, though you did dispatch those poor fools." He sneered at the bodies on the ground.

"Who are you?" asked Ducasien.

"Ah, this one can speak. You have a stronger will than the others. My spell was meant to freeze all muscles, including your throat. See?" The young man spun and lifted his right hand so that the palm faced the sky and a single finger pointed. Inyx watched in silence as one of her fighters choked to death. She saw the skin about his neck turn red and fingers marks appeared where no one touched him. He let out a final gasp and died, purple tongue lolling from his mouth. He did not sag to the ground, however. He remained standing.

"Amazing the control I had over that one," said the mage.

"He refused to relax, even in death." The young man clapped his hands and the dead guerrilla fell face forward to the ground.

Inyx judged the distance and wondered if she could strike before the mage realized she was not similarly paralyzed.

"My lord Patriccan had worried that such an attack might take place on this garrison. The garrison commander had grown lax. He has been punished." The mage smiled. "As severely as some of his soldiers, I see."

The mage walked back and forth through the frozen fighters until he came to Inyx.

"You're a comely wench to be with such an outlaw band. Are you their whore? Do they all use you?"

Ducasien roared and stepped forward, blade rising sluggishly. The spell did not contain him fully, but he had drawn attention to himself. The mage frowned. His lips moved silently and Ducasien froze as solidly as any of the other men.

"Why didn't my spell work on you? It must be more than a matter of will," he mused. The mage's eyes widened. "You're a traveler from along the Road."

He spun and looked into Inyx's brilliant blue eyes. "You, too!"

Inyx lunged and caught the mage in the mouth with her sword point. He gurgled and then spat blood around the steel blade. She recovered and lunged again. The mage already lay dead on the ground, a look of intense surprise permanently etched on his face. The instant he died, Nowless and the others shook the effect of the spell.

"He held us, he did. One man held us all!" Nowless stared at the dead sorcerer. "I had heard of such, but did not believe. How is this possible?" he asked Inyx.

"Never mind that. We've got to get out of here. This one's death might have alerted others."

Ducasien stared at her. "You weren't affected by his spell. Why not?"

The dark-haired woman had no answer for that, but she guessed it had something to do with her close association with Lan Martak. They had shared more than one another's bodies. During their most intimate moments their minds had meshed perfectly, flowing, melting together in a way she had never before experienced. Some of his magical ability — protection — might have lingered.

"Marktown is ours!" she shouted, drowning out further questions. "Prepare for the assault on their fort!"

Inyx did not mention the mage they knew to be in the fort — and now she knew the mage's name. Patriccan. Kiska k'Adesina's pet sorcerer. Inyx had clashed with Patriccan before and the other mage had turned tail and fled.

But Lan Martak had been beside her then. What would happen now when she faced a master sorcerer?

CHAPTER SEVEN

"There are evil stirrings," said Lan Martak. He wiped the sweat off his forehead with his sleeve and continued to stare through the empty doorway in Brinke's study. The woman denied having formal training as a mage, but Lan felt the power within her. He reached out and found his dancing light mote familiar and pulled it close to him, teasing it, coaxing it to spin and whirl in front of Brinke. At the precise instant, Lan released it and let it explode within Brinke.

The blonde arched her back and threw her hands upward. Her head tossed from side to side and piteous moans escaped her lips. Lan did not worry; she was in no physical danger. What menaced them both lay through the archway.

Claybore.

"I have some small control of it," Brinke muttered between clenched teeth. "It is so close. So very, very close."

"There!"

Lan leaned forward and applied his own scrying spells to the strangely formulated one intuitively used by Brinke. A kaleidoscopic pattern churned in the archway and then settled down into a perfect three-dimensional image of Claybore.

"Kill him!" Brinke cried. Her hands clutched the arms of the chair so hard that her knuckles turned white. She half rose and leaned forward, eyes turned into pools of utter hatred.

"Be calm," Lan said soothingly. "This is only a picture of Claybore, not the flesh-and-blood reality." He snorted derisively. "If you can even call him flesh and blood."

Lan studied the image as it moved about on mechanical legs. They worked more smoothly than the prior ones and gave the mage better mobility. But it wasn't the clockwork motion that drew Lan's full attention. The skull showed renewed signs of cracking. The nose hole had several large fractures radiating from it, and in the back of the skull Lan spotted tiny triangular-shaped craters resulting from long cracks intersecting.

"What's wrong with his arms?" asked Brinke.

"They don't seem to be well-hinged, do they?" Lan noted the looseness of the swing, the almost uncontrolled swaying movement. Claybore barely held himself together. When he turned and seemed to face directly at Lan and Brinke, it became all the more apparent.

"His chest!" gasped Brinke.

Lan smiled without humor. He had been responsible for ripping the Kinetic Sphere from Claybore's chest and sending it bouncing along the Cenotaph Road. He had no clear idea where he had discarded it, but it was no longer beating heartlike in the sorcerer's chest. Any small advantage he could garner might prove the difference between winning and losing the battle to come.

Lan's attention wandered a little. He remembered what the Resident of the Pit had said about the Pillar of Night. He shook free of the memory of that ebony, light-sucking column reaching to the very sky. Once he began thinking of it, Lan found it impossible to consider anything else. Perhaps that was its power. To have his thoughts tangled up at an awkward time might mean his death.

Deep down in his heart, his living, beating, flesh heart, Lan Martak did not believe he was immortal. Claybore had said he was and the Resident had intimated it, but Lan had to think otherwise. His powers still grew and would one day match Claybore's, but that day was still in the future. He could not be immortal. Impossible.

"The visual part of the scrying is complete," Lan said. "One more small adjustment and we can spy on him. But do not utter a word. The connection will be two-way. We can see while he cannot, but both Claybore and we will be able to hear."

Brinke nodded understanding. She settled down into her chair, grey eyes fixed on the scene captured under the arch.

Lan performed the final spell.

". . . send Patriccan immediately," Claybore said. "It seems that matters on that world have reached a crisis stage."

"Immediately, master," said a uniformed officer. The woman bowed deeply and backed away, leaving Claybore. The mage sat at a table, elbows resting on the top and fingers peaked just under a jawless, bony mouth. Claybore held the pose for a moment, then laughed.

He rose and pulled out charts. Lan studied them over the mage's shoulder, memorizing the details. Claybore's headquarters were on the other side of the world and at a port city easily reached by either ship or caravan. For Lan it would be a month's journey or more, but Claybore would never know his adversary crept up on him.

"Claybore!" came the shout. "Here!"

Lan spun and saw Kiska standing behind him. He had been so intent on Claybore's map that he had not heard her enter the room. Lan tried to silence her, but the damage had been done.

The ghastly parody of a human jerked about on his clockwork legs. One spastic hand lifted and pointed toward Lan and Brinke. The kaleidoscope patterns returned to the doorway and then faded.

"As I thought. Welcome, Martak, Brinke. And my ever-loyal commander Kiska k'Adesina. How fare you all?"

"He sees us," gasped Brinke.

"But of course I do, Lady Brinke. I am a mage second

to none. Kiska's outburst alerted me. I knew instantly that someone spied upon me. It required no huge mentation to decide that it had to be Martak. While your scrying spells are interesting, they lack subtlety."

"Release me, Claybore. Do not hold me a prisoner to your magics any longer." Brinke's face reddened and Lan saw the beauty erased by the intense emotional storm wracking her.

"Release you from what, my lovely Brinke? That little geas I placed upon you? Don't be silly. You have no idea what it will do. Or when."

"I'll kill you!"

Claybore's mocking laughter filled the chamber. It penetrated like a knife and even sent one of the omnipresent demon-powered cleaning units scuttling away in fear. Lan had listened to the byplay and knew it was for his benefit. All the while Claybore boasted and taunted, Lan summoned his energies. He had thought to rest before this confrontation, but he saw now that he would never be more prepared.

The entire wall vanished as Lan hurled one of his fireballs. The green sphere exploded and melted stone and brick on Lan's side of the spell gate. On Claybore's side maps and papers strewn about the tables ignited and a superheated wind blew against the sorcerer's skull. New cracks appeared, but Claybore seemed not to notice. Claybore's quick hand gestures dropped Lan into inky blackness.

He panicked, remembering the whiteness between worlds. Then he found his light mote and used it to guide him from the pitch black hole and into the sun. Panic would destroy him; calm would allow him to prevail. The two mages fought constantly, striving for advantage.

"Let me help," urged Brinke. "Use me however you can to destroy him!"

"Yes," mocked Kiska, "use her. As if you hadn't already."

Lan dared not silence either of them. He needed full concentration to counter the increasingly devious spells Claybore threw at him. And his own grew in complexity.

Mere power would not suffice. There had to be artifice, also.

"You are not making any headway, Martak."

"Nor are you, Claybore."

"I feel no need to. After all, you are the challenger. You have to unseat me."

"You're no king and I'm no usurper," Lan shot back. He molded his light familiar into a slender needle, the tip of which burned with eye-searing intensity. At the proper instant it would be launched directly for Claybore's skull. Split that bone monstrosity and Lan thought Claybore's power would fade.

"You misjudge our positions."

"Lan!" screamed Brinke.

A rustle of velvet and leather from behind told Lan that Kiska had again tried to knife him in the back. He watched her carefully enough at most times, but when dealing with Claybore he left himself open. As much as he wanted to destroy her, swat her as he would an insect, Lan simply couldn't. It seemed that, with every spell he cast, his love for the woman grew.

Claybore's laughter filled his ears.

"Ah, darling Kiska has again tried and failed. She will succeed one day. But I am not too worried about that. I have other traps laid for you, Martak. You will enjoy them, I'm sure."

"Goodbye, Claybore."

Lan Martak launched the magical needle with all the power locked within him.

Claybore again laughed. Lan sensed rather than saw Claybore slip aside at the last possible instant. And Lan felt himself being pulled forward with the needle. He followed it between worlds and onto another. Only quick reflexes saved him from a nasty spill. He had emerged in thin air some ten feet off the ground. Lan doubled up and rolled and came to his feet.

Beside him stood a dazed Kiska k'Adesina.

He looked around. This was a fair world, but one he'd

never set foot on before. Claybore had outmaneuvered him again. But why?

"Why do you fear this Patriccan?" asked Ducasien.

"I fear his magic, not the man," Inyx answered. She quickly outlined the battles that had raged outside Wurrna on a faraway world and how Patriccan had taken part. "He is skilled and one of Claybore's finest surviving sorcerers. Without him Claybore wouldn't have been able to conquer nearly as many worlds as fast as he has."

"We do not fear him," Nowless said staunchly.

"You should," said Julinne, speaking for the first time in days. "I see only snatches of the future and it is grim. Many, many die. I cannot tell individuals but the land is afloat in blood."

"Now then, good lady, are you really needing the sight to predict that?" scoffed Nowless.

"Patriccan is responsible for many deaths," Julinne said. "There are others, potent others. Mages whose power is so incredible I cannot comprehend it."

"They oppose us at the fort?" asked Ducasien, worried for the first time. "We have adequate fighters"—he looked at Inyx for confirmation—"but spells are rare on this world. Julinne's the only one with a talent worth mentioning."

"Shork can conjure fire from his able fingers," said Nowless. Even as the man spoke he knew how inadequate that sounded. "Perhaps he can learn to do more."

"Before the battle? Hardly," said Inyx. "We have the advantage tactically. Can we still assume we have the element of surprise on our side?"

"No," said Ducasien. "With mages inside the fort? A scrying spell or some infernal ward spell would alert them to our attack long before the main body of fighters arrived. We will have to postpone the battle until they no longer have all these mages available."

"I, for one, have no desire to be turned into a newt, don't you know?" Nowless crossed his arms over his broad chest and glowered.

"I did not say we lacked sorcerers. I said there were many engaged in the battle."

"Now what's it you're really meaning to say?" demanded Nowless. "Are you saying Shork's going to give us the magical cover we need to sneak up on those barstids?"

"Wait." Inyx took Julinne's hand in hers. "Can you see the faces of the mages in the battle?"

A tiny nod.

"One is rat-faced and looks as if he'd just sucked on a bitter root?"

Another nod.

"And another has brown hair, is well built and is accompanied by a small, bright point of light?"

"You have the vision, too?" asked Julinne.

"Lan will somehow come to our aid," she said to Ducasien. "How he found us, I can't say. But he did!"

Ducasien turned and stalked off. Inyx said to Julinne, "Thank you. This is very important. It might mean the difference between success and failure." Inyx bent forward and lightly kissed the other woman on the cheek, then hurried after Ducasien.

She overtook him just as he reached the spot where they'd pitched a small tent.

"Don't be so crackbrained," she said, grabbing his sleeve.

He jerked free of her grip and faced her. "It's always Martak this and Martak that. If he'd been with us, the mage wouldn't have been able to paralyze us. How do you know Julinne's vision is accurate? We've never been able to verify a thing she's said. I think you *want* Martak to be there. In spite of all he's done to you, you *want* to see him again. So do it and be damned!"

"Ducasien, please, wait."

She dropped to hands and knees and followed Ducasien into the tent. There was hardly enough room for the pair of them. It hadn't mattered before.

"We cannot defeat Patriccan without a mage of surpassing power. Neither of us is able to conjure even the simplest of spells. Give us swords and we can fight the best Claybore has in his legion, but against a mage? Forget it." Inyx slumped and rolled onto her back, staring up into the blank green fabric of the tent.

Ducasien said nothing as he lay on his pallet, similarly staring upward. Inyx soon felt his hand atop hers, squeezing gently. She turned and looked into the man's eyes.

"I don't want to lose you," Ducasien said.

"You won't hold me this way."

"He . . ."

Inyx reached over and silenced him with a slender finger against his lips. "Don't speak of him. Not now. The battle is set and we must be ready in an hour."

Ducasien lifted himself up on an elbow and kissed Inyx. She returned it with mounting fervor and soon, in the confines of the tent, they made love.

But Inyx thought not of Ducasien. Her mind rattled with memories of Lan Martak.

"They have gathered just for us," gloated Ducasien. "One swift thrust and they are ours. The power of the grey-clads on this world will be broken."

Inyx wasn't so sure. She looked down at the fort. They had successfully raided it before. Nowless's poison had killed more than half the soldiers, but this victory was short-lived. The commander had called in troops from distant posts to recoup the lost position here.

"Nowless has everything in readiness," said Ducasien. He smiled wickedly as he pointed out the traps and said, "The boulders will smash through the side of the fort and leave them vulnerable to the archers and slingers."

"There's no question that the boulders will do the trick?" asked Inyx. She spoke only to keep her mind off her true worries. Ducasien had had little contact with Claybore's sorcerers and the power of magic. The woman had no desire to face the kinds of spells that might be thrown against their forces.

"The explosive Nowless uses in the pebble-slingers has been mined and planted in appropriate amounts. Fear naught.

All will go well." Ducasien put his arm around her in an attempt to be comforting. Inyx refused to allow herself to relax.

"They have gathered," she said. A last company of grey-clads rode into the fort. "Their meeting begins."

"Their death begins now," said Ducasien. He lifted his arm and gave Nowless the signal. Bass rumblings shattered the still air and caused huge clouds of white smoke and dust to rise. Through the veiling curtain came ponderous boulders, rolling slowly at first, then with greater speed. Nowless had aimed well. Two boulders missed the fort entirely; six more crashed into the wood wall and broke it to splinters.

The legionnaires in the fort boiled forth, swords in hand. Ducasien gave another signal. Clouds of arrows arched up and landed among the soldiers, killing many. A second signal. The slings whirred and hissed and sent forth their tiny pellets of explosive. Against the massive wooden fort walls, these pellets were useless; against humans they took a deadly toll.

"They've taken cover," said Inyx. "We must go down and engage them if we are to wipe them out entirely."

"Another round of boulders," said Ducasien. Explosions, another pair of huge rocks crushing their way through the interior of the fort, disarray among the grey-clads within.

Inyx gave the command for their band to charge down the hill and engage the soldiers. All the distance down the hill she saw arrows arcing overhead to keep the greys in confusion. But Inyx still worried, even though their plan had worked perfectly to this point.

The mage. Where was he?

Inyx saw Patriccan just as she and fifty sword-waving guerrillas reached the breached wall of the fort. The sorcerer walked out, hands hidden in thick folds of his long brown robe. A slight smile danced on his lips. He felt the battle had been won.

"I have expected you," he said. His voice carried strangely over the distance. Inyx heard him as clearly as if he whispered in her ear.

"Surrender!" Inyx yelled to the mage. "Your time on this world is past.".

"Oh?"

A flight of arrows buried itself in the ground around the mage. He deflected the vicious broadheads from his own body but apparently cared little for saving the soldiers. Another dozen of them died near him. But the mage's hands continued working their spells. Inyx saw the air turning hazy in front of Patriccan. And behind, up on the hill where Nowless commanded, came deafening explosions.

"Never use the mystical exploding rock against a mage," Patriccan said, as if lecturing a class of dimwits. "It is too easily turned against you."

"Inyx," gasped Ducasien. "All the slingers are dead."

"Yes, all died. They foolishly carried their projectiles in pouches around their waists. I daresay most were blown in half." Patriccan smiled malevolently and continued, "Now it is your time to die."

He raised his hand to cast the spell. Inyx stood stolidly, awaiting death. She had come far and had wished for a better end than this. The least she could do was meet her fate with courage.

Patriccan finished the spell but nothing happened. Confused, he tried another. And another and still another.

"What's wrong?" demanded Ducasien. "Forget your chants?"

Patriccan shook his head and stared at his hands, as if accusing them of high crimes.

Inyx clapped hands over her ears to protect them from the shrill whistle of an air elemental. She twisted about and saw the lightning-laced haze surging through the darkening sky, plummeting down directly for Patriccan.

The mage saw the danger and began defensive spells. Only great skill prevented the elemental from ripping him limb from limb. As it was, Patriccan fought for his very life. The tide of battle had turned in a split second.

"Kill them. Kill the greys!" shouted Inyx. "Do it while we can!"

The soldiers fell easy prey to their naked swords. But Inyx kept one eye on Patriccan and his battle with the elemental. He struggled to escape and couldn't. And there was no way an ordinary mage could hope to either summon or disrupt an elemental.

"Who sent it?" asked Ducasien, coming to stand beside Inyx.

She shook her head. It had to be Lan Martak, but she found it difficult to believe.

The air elemental winked out of existence. Replacing it was the figure she had grown to hate.

"Claybore!"

"Ah, the cast in the little drama has gathered. Fine." The dismembered mage turned to Patriccan and studied his bruised, broken body. "He is the worse for his encounter with Martak's airborne ally. Where is Martak?"

"Here, Claybore." Thunder sounded and shock waves rolled across the clearing. Emptiness had been replaced by two figures. Lan Martak strode up. "You brought me here, for whatever reason."

"How melodramatic an entrance," said the dismembered sorcerer. "And the capable Commander k'Adesina is with you," continued Claybore, as if Lan had not even spoken. "How are you, my dear?"

Lan's entire body began glowing green as he mustered his sorcerous powers. Claybore laughed and said, "This is the moment. I have the edge now, Martak. Before, you eluded me. Not now. You will cease to exist now!"

The wall of spells erected by the two lifted all the others and carelessly tossed them away. Inyx landed heavily, bruising her shoulder. Ducasien fell into a tree some yards distant. The others of their attack force hobbled and dragged themselves away.

Even Kiska k'Adesina had been discarded by the casual blast of magics.

Inyx got to her feet and drew her dagger. The brief excursion through the air had cost her the sword. Eyes narrowed, she stalked Kiska.

"Lan might not be able to deal with you, but I can!" Inyx drove the sharp point of the dagger down squarely for Kiska's back, but the woman managed to sidestep the blow. They locked together and wrestled to the ground.

"He loves me," taunted Kiska. "You have lost him forever."

"Claybore's spell forces him to love you," Inyx spat out. She tried to bury her teeth in Kiska's neck and failed. They rolled over, with Kiska coming out on top, knees pinning Inyx's shoulders to the ground. Inyx winced in pain from her injury.

"Oh? And why does Lan sleep with the Lady Brinke? Is this more of Claybore's magic?"

"Who?"

Kiska made a small gesture. A picture took form just in front of Inyx's eyes. She saw a lovely, tall blonde woman slowly slipping out of a purple robe to stand naked before Lan Martak. A smile crossed Lan's lips as he began pulling free the laces on his tunic.

"No! It's a lie." Even as she spoke, Inyx knew what she witnessed was a true rendering of a scene that had happened.

"More?" Kiska laughed as the scene played faster than normal, complete to its finish in less than a minute. "There were other times. He has abandoned you, slut. He has left you to die on this backwater world. And die you will!"

Inyx's mind raced. How had this scene been reconstruced? Magically. Did Kiska control any spells? No. Who did? Claybore!

"You try to weaken my will," Inyx said. She twisted against her bad shoulder, then rocked in the other direction, unseating Kiska. They rolled over and over, struggling for dominance.

Both were sent tumbling once more by a wave of heat from where the real battle took place. Lan and Claybore were locked in a furious fight so intense it crossed worlds and returned to boil the very ground beneath their feet. Neither mage noticed. Both vied for supremacy by using every magical trick at their command.

Inyx saw Lan being forced back, yielding, slowly being crushed by the imponderable weight of magics on him.

"Fight, Lan!" she cried. "Stop him!"

She had no idea if her words cheered the mage or if he reached down and found some inner resource that he'd missed. His defense strengthened. He forced Claybore back. Inyx saw the disembodied sorcerer begin to waver. His arms flopped loosely now, as if they would spring from his torso. Even his bone-white skull began cracking.

"He's losing," she whispered in awe. For the first time since she and Lan had walked the Road together, she had the hope that Claybore would be decisively defeated.

Even Kiska k'Adesina watched, her face ashen with the realization that her master might lose.

As suddenly as the shift in power came, another replaced it. Inyx gasped and struggled for breath. Invisible fingers closed about her windpipe.

"She dies, Martak," bragged Claybore. "I will kill the slut."

Inyx fell to hands and knees, panting harshly when the invisible fingers left her throat. Lan had broken Claybore's spell. She looked up in silent thanks. But the gratitude turned to anger when she realized that Claybore had only used her as a diversion for his real attack.

Kiska stood upright, caught between transparent planes crushing the life from her body. She visibly flattened as Claybore applied more and more magical pressure. Her face contorted with the pain of being smashed to bloody pulp. Her brown eyes looked beseechingly at Lan Martak. The young mage paled when he saw the woman's predicament.

"I...I can't fight him and save her. Not at the same time," moaned out Lan Martak.

"Kill Claybore!" shrieked Inyx. "Stop him and you'll stop his spells."

"She dies," cut in Claybore. "I will kill her before you can penetrate my barrier."

Lan fought to drive his light mote through Claybore's protective spells. He failed. And every moment he dallied, more and more life fled from Kiska's body.

"Don't save her, Lan. Kill Claybore!" Inyx's words fell on deaf ears.

Lan Martak turned his full power to saving Kiska.

Claybore broke free. "I almost had you, Martak," said the sorcerer. "I thought this would be the final battle. I erred. But next time. *Then* I will be ready for you. *Then* you die!"

Claybore wavered and *popped!* away, transport spells stolen from Lan carrying him from the world.

"I had him. He...he was weakening," said Lan in a shaky voice. "He would have succumbed. Not even Terrill could best Claybore, and I had him. I *had* him!"

"You unutterable fool," snapped Inyx. "You let him go. And for what? Her?"

Kiska k'Adesina sneered at Lan's weakness. But the power of Claybore's infernal geas grew with every use of magic. Lan Martak had no choice but to protect the woman he loved—and hated.

"You fool," repeated Inyx.

All Lan could do was agree. He held out his opened arms, beckoning to Kiska.

CHAPTER EIGHT

Claybore limped along, his mechanical right leg refusing to function properly. He stopped and stared into the cog-wheeled device and saw that one of the magical pinpoints of energy had been extinguished. From deep within his skull's empty eye sockets came a tentative pink glow that firmed into a rod of the purest ruby light. It lashed forth to the offending spot on his leg. The metal turned viscid and flowed; Claybore's death beams winked out before the metal deformed.

"There," he said. "Repaired. But damn that Martak. I should have my own legs instead of these pathetic creations."

"Master, we failed," came a weak voice. Claybore swiveled about to face Patriccan. The journeyman mage clung to a tree trunk a few feet away. All blood had rushed from his face, leaving him with a pasty complexion. His eyes looked like two dark holes burned into a linen sheet. In spite of the apparent weakness, the mage had a feverish air about him, one approaching desperation.

"Failed?" roared Claybore. "How dare you say we failed?"

"Master, we did not destroy Martak. Or the others."

"Forget the others. They are nothings. They are ciphers in this equation. Martak is all." Claybore calmed. "While it is true we did not triumph totally, still we did not lose all, either."

Patriccan's appearance belied that boast.

"Martak's strength surprised me, but I was not unprepared to deal with it. There is dissension in our enemy's ranks now. And I still have my most potent weapon aimed at his heart." Claybore chuckled at the pun. "Kiska will sow the seeds of discord and, when the time is ripe, she will destroy Martak."

"We should have defeated him," said Patriccan, sliding down the tree to sit between two large roots. "I lost all power when he sent the air elemental for me."

"You are a weakling," Claybore said without apparent malice.

"Is it enough having them fighting among themselves?" asked the lesser sorcerer.

Claybore did not respond for some time. Finally came the single word, "Yes."

Patriccan was hardly satisfied with his defeat. Martak had been so strong!

"Find a living creature and bring it to me," ordered Claybore. The dismembered mage went to the lip of a well and peered into the infinite ebony depths. He chuckled at the thought of who lay trapped within. Claybore's ruby beams lashed forth and stirred the blackness, like a spoon stirring soup. Tiny ripples flowed and subsided.

"Here, master." Patriccan limped up with a small doe. The creature kicked out with hooves and tried to wiggle free. The mage held it magically and gave the poor beast no chance to escape.

A wave of Claybore's hand sent the doe tumbling into the well. A greeting surge of darkness enveloped the deer and swallowed it whole.

"Resident of the Pit, are you there?" called out Claybore. "I would speak to you."

"I am here."

"You have failed, Resident. You know that now. You saw how easily we defeated Martak and the others."

"Martak lives."

"But what good will he be? His friends have abandoned him. Inyx and the insect Krek are needed—and they shun him."

"I have seen." The Resident of the Pit's voice rumbled in a basso profundo.

"And," went on Claybore, warming to his bragging, "my commander's influence over him grows every time he uses even the most minor of spells against me."

"That is so."

"Even Brinke's power will not free him. I use her to further entangle him. Inyx will never again support Martak, not after Kiska informed her of Martak's liaison with Brinke."

"I have seen all this. Why do you summon me, Claybore?"

"You, a god, asking a question like that? Come, come, Resident, you know why. I want you to suffer. I want you to know the glory of my triumph. I want you to know that you have failed. Your pawn Lan Martak is worthless to you now."

"There will be others," said the Resident of the Pit. "I have nothing but time."

"Martak will be removed soon," said Claybore. "When he is gone, I will augment my power and finally become a god. I will see to it that you never die. You will live in this dimensionless limbo forever, forgotten by your worshippers and doomed to endlessly watch and wait—for nothing!"

"Even if you do achieve your ambition, I will find a way to die. I grow so weary of this existence."

"It must be terrible," Claybore said insincerely. "Seeing everything, knowing everything, and being unable to do anything about it."

"Release me, Claybore. I am nothing to you. Destroy me. I want to die."

"A god can never die. You know that." Claybor laughed and let the Resident of the Pit slowly drift back into the timeless boredom of his existence.

"What now, master?" asked Patriccan.

"We recover, then approach Martak once more. This time we go in peace, not in battle." Claybore chuckled to himself. "Perhaps this time we will destroy him totally."

"This is victory?" asked Inyx. She stared at the battlefield and shivered in reaction. She had a bloodthirsty side to her nature, but seeing such carnage was not to her liking. It was one thing to do battle with your foe, hand to hand, sword to sword, and best him. The wholesale slaughter of the grey-clads by the arrows had been bad—the sight of all the slingers blown in half by Patriccan's reversal of the spell used in the explosive pellets sickened her.

"Of course it is," said Nowless. "Don't you see how they have lost? Their fort is well nigh destroyed and all the soldiers are dead or put to rout. Their power over us is broken."

Inyx looked at Ducasien, who shared her concern. Almost seven hundred had died this day. Few of them had died in a manner either she or Ducasien would consider honorable.

Inyx saw Lan and Kiska nearby. The pair argued. She found no solace in that. If it hadn't been for Lan's inability to let Kiska k'Adesina suffer, Claybore would have been defeated and the long, hard road they had followed would have been vindicated. But Lan Martak had succumbed to Kiska's pleas and Claybore had escaped.

He had not reached the point of his hatred for the woman to overcome the compulsion spell placed on him.

What bothered the dark-haired woman the most was knowing that Lan would not have saved her had she been the one in trouble. Claybore had used the same spells on her, and Inyx had felt the invisible fingers choking the life from her body. Lan's attack on the master sorcerer had been unabated, but the instant Claybore shifted his attack to Kiska, Lan had ceased fighting and had fought only to save Kiska.

"He loves her," said Ducasien.

"He does not," Inyx snapped back. "It's some damned geas Claybore put on him. Lan knows it, but the compulsion spell is too subtle for him to break."

"That is a convenient excuse," said Ducasien.

"It is not an excuse. It's the truth. There's no other explanation for the way Lan acts around her. She is an avowed enemy. He killed her husband and she has tried to murder him repeatedly."

"There's no accounting for tastes, especially when it comes to love."

Inyx started to say something further to Ducasien, then thought better of it. The man was new to the Road and the ways of mages. He had no clear-cut idea what a tiny spell might do—or the power of a major one. Still, even knowing how adept and cunning Claybore was did not ease the pain Inyx felt at this moment.

Both Kiska and Lan were under the compulsion spell, but Kiska slipped free at all the worst times to attempt to kill Lan. Inyx wondered if Claybore's intent was physical death or just a wounding, a weakening at the precisely opportune second. Claybore battled for the most ambitious of all goals: godhood.

"This world is freed of the grey-clads, at least for the time being," Inyx said, changing the subject. "Nowless had better organize a new government if he wants to keep the countryside from falling into chaos."

"Nowless isn't much of an administrator," said Ducasien.

"Or much else, if you ask me," Inyx said. She blinked when she realized what Ducasien really meant.

"Why not?" the man said. "This is a lovely world. We can stay and rule."

"You would be king?"

"Perhaps not king, but something significant. When I left Leponto I never thought of settling down and finding a single spot to live. Now the idea appeals to me. It becomes even more beguiling if I—we—were in positions of power."

"I have never considered it," said Inyx, frowning. She had walked the Road for years and relished the thrill of adventure. But all things must come to pass. Was it time to cease her aimless ramblings?

With Ducasien?

Lan Martak walked up, Kiska trailing behind. The woman had a smirk on her face that contrasted with Lan's glum expression.

"What do you want?" demanded Inyx.

"To speak with you. Alone."

"Oh? Think you can leave your precious Kiska for such a long time?"

"Don't be more of a bitch than you have to, Inyx. This is important."

"I am sure it is."

Lan looked at her, pain in his eyes. "I can't help myself. I've tried. Every spell I've ever known or heard of, I've tried over and over. Claybore did not attain such power without being very, very good at his magics."

"And you're some tyro from a backwater world. Is that it?"

"Yes, Inyx, that's so." The hurt in his words softened Inyx's mood.

"You left Krek to fend for himself. And you've repeatedly chosen her over me. Oh, Lan, why? Why did it have to turn out this way?" Inyx stiffened when she felt the mental reaching out. She and Lan were bound together as one again—almost. The final link never formed. Inyx let the tears welling in her eyes run down her cheeks. Once more she had been cheated. The promise had not been fulfilled.

"I need you," he said simply.

Inyx looked past Lan to where Ducasien and Kiska stood in stony silence. Ducasien fingered the hilt of his sword. Inyx knew the man well enough by now to know he considered drawing and killing; Inyx also knew that Ducasien would never succeed. Lan's magics were quicker than any sword.

Lan Martak. Ducasien.

"Lan," she said, "I've made my decision. I can't continue with you. Ducasien and I are going to stay here. There's so much to be done. The people are good but unorganized. If they are ever to be able to fight off another wave of the grey soldiers, there has to be a strong army."

"You and Ducasien will rule here, then?"

"Not rule," she said, loathing the idea of having life and death over others, "but advise. We are needed. *I* am needed."

"But . . ."

Inyx cut him off with a wave of her hand. "Kiska has told me much that you'd probably not care to have related. Does the name Brinke mean anything to you?"

Lan frowned. Inyx saw anger building within him, but it wasn't directed at her. If Claybore's geas had not been so damnably strong, Lan Martak would have reduced Kiska to a smoldering pile of lard. Instead, he shook impotently, unable to act against her.

"It's true, then," said Inyx. Infinite tiredness washed over her like the ocean's pounding surf. "That was no spell of Claybore's doing, I'm sure."

"What would you have me do? You deserted me. You went off with him."

"I deserted you?" Inyx's eyebrows shot upward in surprise. Then she laughed. "We have nothing more to say to one another, Lan. Whatever understanding there was between us has fled."

"Inyx. . . ."

She pushed past him and returned to stand beside Ducasien, hand on his arm.

"Lan, oh, Lan," called out Kiska. "Are we leaving soon? These are such dreary people. So inhospitable."

"Be quiet," he said, but there was no fire in his voice. Kiska laughed at him.

Nowless and Julinne stood to one side, confused. They whispered between themselves, obviously debating the motives of these people who had saved them from the grey-clads. Finally, Nowless shrugged and stepped forward.

"We celebrate this night," he said. "We want you to be our honored guests, don't you know."

"Thanks, Nowless. We accept," Ducasien said before Lan could answer.

Lan nodded assent. He jerked away when Kiska tried to

lock her arm through his. In silence more fitting to the defeated than the victors, they trudged back into the rocky hills and Nowless's camp to begin the celebration.

"You're so good to me, Lan," cooed Kiska. She spoke the words the instant she knew Inyx was within earshot. From the disheveled brown hair and the flushed expression on the woman's face, Inyx had no trouble guessing what Kiska and Lan had been doing.

She repressed a shudder thinking of that woman in Lan's arms.

"Nowless is ready to begin the feast," said Inyx, ignoring Kiska the best she could.

"We'll be there shortly," answered Lan, lacing up the front of his tunic. Kiska laughed delightedly at the hurt she gave both Lan and Inyx. The young mage went over in his head all the spells and counters he had learned. For the millionth time he went over them and found nothing to release him from Claybore's geas. The pure torture was knowing he was under the spell and unable to do anything but abide by it.

He fastened his sword-belt around his waist and left Kiska where they had been given bedrolls and a small tent. Lan started toward the fire and the celebrants, then paused. The feast would continue for some time with or without him. He climbed up onto the rocks and found a tiny upjut on which to stand and survey the land.

"A good world," he said softly. "Inyx has done well in choosing it. That spot yonder would make a good farm. Plenty of water from the river, but with little chance of being flooded out should it overflow its banks. And the village—Marktown—is close by. A good market for crops."

He pictured himself in the fields, tending the crops, weeding, joyously performing the backbreaking labor. It was a life for which he had been destined until he had fled his home world by walking the Cenotaph Road. Since then Lan's life had been out of control—out of his control. He was nothing more than a pawn in a celestial game, being moved from one conflict to another. Lan didn't even know for certain who the players were, but he had strong suspicions.

"Resident of the Pit, you have not done well by me. Not at all."

"No, the fallen god hasn't," came the words from behind him. Lan had already felt the magical stirrings of a shift from one world to another. His own ward spells were firmly in place. The dancing light mote strained to launch itself against Claybore, but Lan held it in check.

"What do you want?" Lan asked. "You have not joined me to share the serenity of this moment."

Claybore laughed. "What you call serenity I find boring. There are none to pay homage to me here. The wind? Why not summon an obedient air elemental? The night? Look into the depths of eternity and find diversion there. I need stimulation, not serenity."

"You want only worshippers."

"Is that so wrong? I deserve it. Of all those along the Road, I am the strongest. It is my destiny to rule."

"I'll stop you."

"Is it truly your destiny to attempt it? Or, as you intimated, are you only doing another's insane bidding? Martak, I have no great love for you . . ."

Lan snorted.

". . . but I will make you an offer unlike any I have granted any other. I will give you half of everything."

"What? Half of the universe?" Lan didn't know whether to laugh or spit.

"Yes," Claybore said earnestly. "I have come to the conclusion that being a god will be like ash on the tongue without strife. If there is none to oppose me, what more intense boredom can there be?"

"I already oppose you."

"But not of your own free will. The Resident of the Pit fills your head with his obsolete teachings. Together we can destroy the Resident and work for our own ends."

"That's what he wants. Why give the Resident surcease?" Lan wondered at this strange offer, then pieces fell together.

"You still fear the Resident of the Pit, but you cannot destroy a god. With my help, you can? Yes," said Lan, understanding bursting upon him now. "With my help you can finally destroy the Resident."

"And gain half the universe for yourself. I need the opposition to make life interesting."

Lan said nothing. There had to be more. Claybore did not make this offer lightly—or honestly.

"It cuts the other way, also," said Claybore. "You are immortal. Without an adversary you will find life impossibly dull. You need me as much as I need you."

"You are evil."

"So you think. From my point of view, you are demented. I offer stability to the worlds along the Road. My rule might not be pleasant, but it will be firm. The petty humans will have a society that fills their need for security. There will be no sudden, unsettling shifts of policy. Even as they hate me, they will cherish what I bring them."

"You bring them slavery."

"I bring them security."

Lan wondered if Claybore truly believed this. Perhaps so. It mattered little. He knew the horrors the disembodied mage would wreak. He and Claybore stood at opposite poles.

But what would Lan do when he triumphed over Claybore and relegated the sorcerer to insignificance? As much as he hated Claybore and all the sorcerer stood for, he had to admit the mage was right. An important element of his life would be gone. No Claybore, no struggle. With the powers at his command, Lan Martak could send worlds spinning from their orbits. He could destroy worlds—and create new ones. No task, major or minor, was beyond his grasp. Where would be the challenge without Claybore?

"You begin to understand," said Claybore. "I offer you half the universe not out of altruism but out of self-interest. I *need* strong opposition, just as you do."

"I will not help you kill the Resident of the Pit."

"But Lan," pleaded Kiska k'Adesina, scrabbling up the

rocks to stand beside him, "think of it! The power! You *must* accept. You have to. I would be a queen of a million worlds. Give me my heart's desire. Accept Claybore's offer."

Lan swallowed hard. He knew what Kiska's only desire was. She wanted revenge on him for what he had done to her. Accepting Claybore's offer only magnified the chances for Kiska to strike.

But. . . .

Lan Martak weakened. He saw the truth in Claybore's words. Without evil there can be no good. To live forever had seemed an awesome attainment once. Now Lan realized how dulling it might become. Who had he met along the Road able to stimulate him as Claybore did, to bring out the finest qualities? He needed a foil of his own caliber as much as the sorcerer needed him.

Eternity was a long, long time. There had to be something diverting. He began to comprehend why the Resident wanted only death.

"No, Lan," came a soft whisper. "Do not listen."

The Resident of the Pit spoke to him.

"How do I know you won't use me to kill the Resident, then double-cross me?" Lan asked.

"You don't." Lan realized this might be one of the few times he received an honest answer from Claybore. "But isn't that what we speak of now? The challenge? The striving?"

"Lan," whispered the Resident of the Pit, "there is more than ruling. You will become like Claybore if you try to force your will on so many worlds. There are other answers. Seek them. Seek them." The Resident's power faded but the memory lingered. Lan swelled with the power radiated from that god-entity's light touch on his mind.

"No," Lan said.

"You are hasty. There is so much I can show you," said Claybore.

Lan stiffened as the night became darker. In the distance he saw a shimmering curtain that parted to reveal a shaft of the purest obsidian black. Radiating spikes crowned it and they began to rotate slowly. The material of the slick-sided tower sucked light and heat away from Lan. He felt himself drawn to the column, drawn and repelled at the same time. All he knew, all he wanted to know, was locked up within that column.

"The Pillar of Night," Claybore said softly. "It is your fate because you have so foolishly denied me."

Lan Martak continued to stare at the vision of the Pillar of Night until Kiska tugged at his arm and pulled him angrily toward the feast. He followed her as if he were in a deep trance.

The Pillar of Night! His destiny—and the universe's.

CHAPTER NINE

"It holds the key to Claybore's defeat," said Lan Martak. "I know it. If I can find out the secret hidden by the Pillar of Night I know I can defeat him."

Inyx stared at Lan from across the campfire. Ducasien's arm rested around her shoulders, and the man's steely stare speared into Lan's very soul. The mage continued with his pleas. He had to make them understand the importance of what he had been shown.

"It is Claybore's weapon, but it can be turned against him. I feel it."

"Then why mention it in *her* presence?" Ducasien glared at Kiska k'Adesina, who sat licking thick grease off her fingers before picking up still another roast haunch. She loudly cracked open a bone and sucked noisily at the marrow, appearing unconcerned that she was the topic of conversation.

"I need your help," said Lan, almost stuttering. He couldn't find the words to make them understand what strain he endured because of Kiska. Inyx knew Claybore had laid the geas on him but they didn't *understand*. They couldn't. They weren't sorcerers.

"Claybore has shown you this Pillar," said Inyx. "If it can be used against him, why show it to you at all?"

"Every time I have seen it, there has been an unsettling power flow from it," explained Lan. "Claybore uses this to unbalance me, to counter my spells. It . . . it's like a riposte. You wait for your opponent to attack, then you parry and lunge."

"The mere sight of this black rock puts you off balance so much?" asked Ducasien. The man's tone told all. He thought Lan lied for his own purposes.

"It's a magical construct, not a real rock. It sucks up light. And the spikes atop it must signify something I have yet to learn."

"Let her tell you. She's Claybore's commander in chief now."

Kiska smiled and finished off a second piece of the roast meat. She tossed the gnawed bones over her shoulder and into the dark. Lan winced when she did this; it was poor camp sanitation. But what did Kiska care? She wouldn't be long on this world, because she knew Lan had to pursue Claybore, wherever the dismembered mage went.

"At least, when she's with me, she commands nothing. Claybore's robbed of her services in that respect."

Ducasien whispered something to Inyx. The dark-haired woman shook her head, then gave in.

"Good night, Lan," Inyx said. "I don't think there's any reason to continue this conversation further."

"You won't help me?" he asked, stricken.

"You don't need us. You made that clear many times over. Your magics are beyond our ken. Let me stay where my weapon—the sword—is adequate."

"The grey-clad soldiers are just pawns. Claybore is the hand moving them, the brain guiding their motion."

"Eliminate enough pawns, Martak," said Ducasien, "and the hand has nothing left to move."

Inyx and Ducasien left the circle of light cast by the

campfire. Lan listened as their boots disturbed tiny pebbles. He heard the sliding of cloth against tent and then soft, intimate sounds that turned him cold inside.

"Let's leave this dreary world, darling Lan," said Kiska. "I tire of those fools."

Lan Martak jerked away from her and stood, his lips already forming the spells to move him—them—back to the world where the Pillar of Night rose like an inky cloud to blot out the very sun. He and Kiska *popped!* away from this world and the victory over the grey-clads and Ducasien and . . . Inyx.

"She spies on us. I am sure of it," said Brinke. "Claybore must know our every word."

Lan had to agree. He and Kiska had returned to this world a week ago and Claybore had thwarted his every scheme, countered his spells with a sureness that came from knowledge.

"Is he able to see into the future?" asked Brinke. "It hardly seems possible. This Julinne's talent is unique in my experience."

"You must be right when you said that Claybore had a source of information within our ranks," said Lan. "But how is it accomplished? I have watched Kiska carefully and have failed to see how she contacts him. The most delicate of ward spells is bypassed. He is cunning, that Claybore."

All of Lan's efforts to engage Claybore in direct battle again had failed. Lan took this to mean that the other sorcerer knew he was the weaker; Lan once saw an arm fall from Claybore's shoulder, only to have the mage reattach it with hasty binding spells. And of the Kinetic Sphere—Claybore's heart—there was no sign. Lan had successfully ripped it from the mage's chest and randomly cast it along the Road. It might take Claybore years to regain it, or centuries, if Lan were lucky.

Until that time, Claybore's powers were diminished. Not much, but perhaps enough. If only Lan could pin Claybore to one spot and make him fight!

"There is so little I can do," said Brinke. The regal, tall blonde folded her hands in her lap and slumped. "My own spells are undeveloped. Until Claybore came, there was scant reason to nurture them. Now it is too late to learn what is needed."

"But Claybore's been here on this world for centuries," said Lan. He frowned. "I don't understand. You make it sound as if he'd only recently come."

"I have never seen this Pillar of Night you speak of. Indeed, I had no idea this world was even visited by travelers along the Road until a few years ago. Claybore and a few of his officers arrived."

"They organized local companies of the greys, then spread their influence," Lan said. "That's the usual pattern. But what was unusual was that Claybore did not leave once his power had been established."

"That is so," she said.

Lan looked at the woman and grew increasingly uncomfortable. He was powerfully attracted to her. While his dalliances with Kiska were not of his choosing, those with Brinke definitely were. And he felt increasingly guilty about them. Kiska winked lewdly and looked the other way, but he knew she had spoken of them to Inyx. And it was Inyx that bothered Lan the most. He had no pretensions of fidelity, either on his or on Inyx's part, but involvement with Brinke put him at a disadvantage.

He still loved Inyx and anything used to push her farther away tore at his guts.

"Claybore," the blonde went on, "controls this world with an iron grip. Few of us have successfully fought him. My family was halved during the first real uprising. We were halved again in number over subsequent skirmishes and only I remain to carry the fight to the mage." Bitterness tinted her words as Brinke remembered the horrors of conflict that she had witnessed.

It was always this way, Lan knew.

"You have managed to keep Claybore at bay," said Lan. "You must have powers you don't realize."

"I have no idea why Claybore hasn't destroyed me as he did the others. Impalement. Beheading. Quartering. He magically tossed my sister high into the air and fed her to an air elemental. She lived for five days before she died." In a voice almost too soft for Lan to hear, Brinke added, "It rained her blood for over an hour."

"There has been overmuch of Claybore's brutality. I have a plan that might work, but I cannot allow Kiska to accompany me. She would report directly to Claybore when she learned what I intend to do."

"She can be kept in a cell for a few days, I think," said Brinke. "With enough blanketing spells around her she won't be able to contact Claybore."

"That's my only hope," said Lan.

Brinke's eyes locked with his again and Lan felt his heart stirring, going out to this lovely, brave woman.

"I am depending on you to hold her," he said.

"Count on me. You must steel yourself to be without her, and that might be worst of all. What is your plan?"

"Not much of one," Lan admitted. He began pacing, unconsciously locking his hands behind his back as he had seen Ducasien do. "The Pillar of Night is the key. I know it. But my ignorance about what it actually is holds me back. Scouting the Pillar is all I can do. With subtle enough magics, I might be able to creep close enough to examine it without Claybore discovering."

"A double," Brinke said suddenly. "We can arrange for a double. Oh, not anyone who can perform the arcane spells you command, but a physical double to walk the battlements and be seen from a distance. I am sure Claybore has spies watching the castle. If we can dupe them for only a few days, that will give you time to reconnoiter."

Lan had little faith in such a deception. Claybore's magics were such that the slightest of spells would reveal the double. But Lan had nothing to lose by trying.

"Do you have someone in mind? I can spin a few spells about him that might confuse any seeing him."

"With a suit of your clothes and some expert makeup,"

said Brinke, "this will work. I know it!"

They discussed the potential for danger to the double for some time. Then their words turned more intimate and Lan forgot his reservations about becoming involved further with this gorgeous, beguiling woman.

He left just before dawn the next day.

Lan sensed the power emanating from the Pillar of Night as if it were a column of intense flame. Even from a hundred miles away, he knew the precise location and homed in toward it. The man longed to use some small spell to propel himself across the distance in the blink of an eye, but he knew this would prove fatal. Stealth was his ally. He had no idea if his double parading around Brinke's castle had fooled anyone or not, but Lan had to believe it had.

He had spent more than ten days in the demon-powered flyer, listening to the hissing of the creature in the back compartment. The demon's continual complaints wore on him; when he didn't effectively silence the demon, the vituperation became worse.

"What a cruel master you are," shrieked the demon through a tiny port just behind Lan's head. "Lady Brinke never flies more than an hour at a time. You tire me."

"You can't tire," said Lan, tired. "Would you have me send you back to the Lower Places?"

"See?" cried the demon. "Threats! You abuse me, then you threaten me when I speak of it. How awful you are!"

"Keep the rotors turning," ordered Lan, seeing that the demon was slacking off again.

"I . . . I can't. Something drains my strength."

Lan started to argue, then felt the waves striking him. Power diminished and he wanted to fall asleep. Only through will power did he keep going.

The Pillar of Night rose up from the plain, a black digit defying him.

"The spikes atop the Pillar," he muttered. Tiny discharges leaped from one to the other. With every spark came new weakness. The closer he flew to the Pillar, the less able he would be.

"I hurt!" complained the demon. "My fingers are blistered and my muscles are over-tired. And I . . . I feel trapped. I must escape this steel prison!" Loud ringings came from the chamber as the demon began scratching at the plates in a vain effort to escape. The binding spells were too adroit.

"Be calm," Lan said. "There's nothing we can do about it. That column frightens me as much as it does you."

"Impossible! I piss on myself in fear! Gladly will I piss on you!"

Lan stared at the Pillar, then pushed down on the flyer's controls and landed at the edge of a forest ringing the base of the magical construct.

"You will stay here," Lan said. "No other can command you."

"You will die in that forest," said the demon. "I'll be lost in this iron pot forever. You can't do this. Oh, you cruel, cruel monster!"

Lan pulled what supplies he had left from the flyer and hoisted them to a pack on his back. The forest disquieted him. Lan tingled as magics began growing. The tree limbs whipped and swung for his face, thorny vines raking his flesh and drawing bloody streaks. The temptation to use his light mote familiar to clear a path dogged his steps, but he fought it down. These were not natural woods; they were Claybore's creation. Any spell used within the perimeters of the woods would alert the sorcerer instantly.

Lan wanted to examine the Pillar of Night carefully before betraying his presence.

But the forest became denser and the plants more aggressive. When Lan camped for the night in a tiny clearing, he built a larger than normal fire to keep the creeping plant life at bay. Even this had little effect; he noticed the trees themselves beginning to circle him, their roots painfully pulling out of the soil, only to burrow back in a spot just a few inches closer.

"There's nothing to fear," he said aloud. The words seemed to hold back the encroaching plants, with their gently waving spined pads and powerfully coiling and uncoiling shoots. Lan put another small log onto the fire; the dancing light both attracted and pushed the plants back. He guessed the warmth and need for photosynthesis drew the trees and smaller plants, but the fear of being burned held them at bay.

"Fear?" he wondered aloud, sitting up and hugging his knees in to his chest. Sleep refused to come. "Do they fear? Do they love? Or are their movements instinctual and only in response to a stimulus?"

He dozed off, only to be awakened by a cold, slippery vine stroking over the back of his neck. Lan came awake instantly, a spell forming on his lips. He caught himself and drew forth his dagger, slashing frantically when the vine began tightening around his left arm. The severed vine pulled back and Lan imagined he heard a piteous howling of pain.

The rest of the night was spent wary and half asleep, no real rest being gained.

Seldom had he been so glad to see sunrise.

He stood and stretched cramped muscles and wiped away an ichorous substance left by the vine when he'd cut it. Lan pushed through the tight circle of trees, some of which were less than two feet apart, and used his sword to hack away the bushes.

He ate a trail breakfast as he walked, not wanting to spend any more time in the forest than necessary. He had only just penetrated the forest; he didn't cherish the idea of spending another night within its boundaries.

Finding a meandering stream of muddy water allowed Lan to make better progress along the banks. Branches formed a canopy above and shut out the cheering sunlight, but the added speed more than made up for the dreary landscape.

"I . . . I can't breathe," Lan gasped out after walking for more than an hour. "The air. Gone stale. No breath. So hard." He started to fall forward when a long, slender vine dropped down and wrapped itself tightly about his right wrist. Long needles shot into his flesh and the pain rocketing into his brain pulled him out of the fog. He screeched in anguish and tried to jerk free. He only succeeded in losing his balance on slippery rocks.

Crashing down to the stream bank, Lan struggled in the vine's grip. He found his knife and slashed awkwardly at the green rope until he cut it in two. The pain kept him working until the sucker pad that had already sampled his blood and the sharp, hollow spines were removed from his wrist.

"Air," he panted, then wondered. The shock of pain had kept him breathing. "There's nothing wrong with the air," he said to himself. "It's a guard spell. That's all it can be."

He hunkered down and forced his lungs to suck in deep draughts of air as he gently probed for the source of the spell. He didn't find it, but took the chance of using a counter. Chanting, softly at first and then with more determination, he worked out a magical pump that would force air into his lungs, even if his chest refused to expand to accept it. In this way Lan hoped to attract little attention to himself—he wasn't opposing the spell but rather working on himself to counter the effects of the spell.

Just as he thought all was again serene, a bloodcurdling scream ripped apart the stillness of the forest.

Lan heard heavy crashing through the thick undergrowth and drew his sword, ready to fight. Without an instant's warning, a heavy body surged through the air directly at him. Lan dropped to one knee, braced the hilt of his sword on the ground, and felt the impact. The blade twisted mightily and almost left his grip, but he held on grimly.

A man—or parts of what had been a man—had perished on his carbon-steel blade.

"Who are you?" Lan asked, pulling his sword from the man's chest. The grotesquely misshapen head belied any claim to humanity. One arm was missing and the legs bent at curious angles. The sword had found the proper spot between ribs to penetrate through to the heart.

Lan could hardly believe that the creature still lived. One torn eyelid waggled up and down to reveal a glassy, bloodshot eye. The other eyelid opened to reveal a gaping cavity where the eyeball had been plucked out.

"Who are you?" asked Lan, kneeling beside the creature. "Let me tell your people where you died."

The raucous laughter welling up from the creature's throat chilled Lan. He stepped away, then used his sword to put the *thing* out of its misery. The wound started under one ear and deeply cut to the other. Lan Martak felt unclean even seeing such a parody of humanity.

"You have this much more to answer for, Claybore," he said. "This foul work has your imprint on it. I know that."

"Oh, yes, of course, of course it is his handiwork. Who else strays into these woods, eh, tell me that, tell me that?"

Lan spun, dropping into an *en garde* stance at the words. A man with arms three times normal size hung from a tree. He had no legs. Swinging back and forth, the man built momentum and reached for another tree limb and moved closer to Lan.

"Who are you? Who by the lowest of the Lower Places was he?" Lan indicatd the pitiful creature sprawled on the ground, still feebly twitching as if life refused to flee even after having heart pierced and throat slit.

"We're all having fun, ever so much fun, yes, fun, fun, fun!"

The half-man whirled and capered about, swinging skillfully from limb to limb and then dropping to the forest floor. He stared up at Lan.

"You're not one of us. You're an interloper. I know all of us. And you're not. One of us. No, no you're not."

Lan swallowed hard and gripped his sword even tighter. He had seen madness in his day. This was a classic case and he had to·deal with it. Had the loss of his legs driven the man insane?

Lan Martak doubted it. Claybore's magical experimentations were more likely to blame.

"Did Claybore try to use your legs for his own?" Lan asked.

"What? Oh, yes, yes! He had to fight me for them. But it wasn't much of a fight. No, not at all. I lost." A huge, salty tear formed at the corner of the man's round, dark eye and dribbled unashamedly down his cheek.

"Get revenge on Claybore," said Lan. "Show me the way

to the Pillar of Night. I would examine it closely. You've seen it, I know. It's near, only a few minutes away. I sense it. But something prevents me from seeing it directly."

"The forest, that's what. The trees block your view." Another big tear rolled down the man's cheek and then anger clouded the once handsome face. "Revenge. I want to get even for what he did to me. Kill you. You're like him. Kill you!"

Lan watched as the legless man rocked forward and pulled his body along on those impossibly powerful arms. The biceps were almost the size of Lan's waist. The strength locked up in that half body presented too great a threat to take lightly.

"I oppose Claybore. I don't want to hurt you."

"Kill!" screamed the man.

Lan gasped in pain as one huge, powerful hand circled his ankle and clamped down. He felt the bones grating against one another. He swung his sword and severed the hand; it continued to cling to his leg. Gorge rising, Lan stumbled back, swinging wildly. The man came on, pulling himself on the spurting stump of his left wrist and his right hand. Sickened beyond compare, Lan lunged and drove the blade directly into the man's throat.

The right hand grabbed the steel blade and broke it, as if it were nothing more than a splinter.

"Kill you," came the words. A tide of crimson followed. The man fell forward, eyes sightlessly staring. Lan held the broken sword in his hand, shocked at how close he had come to dying.

He turned and became violently sick to his stomach. When the nausea passed he followed his sensing toward the Pillar. Scouting had been a good idea. He hadn't realized Claybore kept his experimental failures in the forest surrounding the base. Lan Martak wasn't sure he wanted to know any more if he had to kill cripples.

"It only gets worse," came quiet words from the shadows at the base of a large boled tree.

"How would you know?" demanded Lan.

CHAPTER TEN

Lan Martak stood and stared and then tried to compose himself. He hardly believed the white-haired man, and yet a ring of truth came through that pushed away any doubts he might have.

"If you are the Terrill who destroyed Claybore, why do you stay here?" Lan indicated the odd forest. He felt the hair on the back of his neck rising at the lack of sound in the woods. No insects chirped or flew. The wind refused to blow through the living, moving leaves and walking plants. Even the odors struck Lan as peculiar. None of the death-turning-to-life smells rose from the floor of the forest. It had an antiseptic odor to it, as if nothing decayed.

"I am bound. Claybore defeated me, even as I bested him." The man sat down on a small rock and cupped his chin in gnarled hands. "Those were days of worth. Now?" He looked around, his washed-out eyes betraying no emotion at all.

"Are you under a geas?" Lan asked eagerly. Terrill was the greatest mage who ever conjured. If anyone could remove the geas Lan suffered, it had to be Terrill. And in return Lan might be able to free the master from his bondage.

"What?" Terrill said, distractedly. "No, no geas. I stay because I have no other place to go."

"I don't understand."

"You haven't seen it, then, have you? No? Come along." Terrill motioned for Lan to follow. The younger mage sucked in his breath when he felt the force of the Pillar of Night growing. They walked directly to it.

"There."

Lan peered through the canopy of leaves and spotted the bulk of the magical column. He tried to move closer and found his feet would not obey.

"This is as close as any can get," said Terrill. "That is Claybore's power."

"Help me fight him. We need you. He has almost put himself back together."

"I did tear him asunder, didn't I?" asked Terrill. "I had forgotten that. There are so many other things to occupy me now. Important things."

"More important than stopping Claybore?" Lan's mind reeled with the concept of any danger being greater.

"Oh, yes, definitely, definitely. Come and I'll show you. Don't be afraid. They won't hurt you."

Terrill led him to a small clearing. "This is my home. Mine and my friends."

Lan stopped at the edge of the clearing and stared. Crude dolls constructed of leaves and twigs, held together with sap and dried mud, stood in neat rows. Terrill went to one and gently stroked over hair made from dead vines.

"She is my favorite, above all others, my most cherished. We have important discussions and, well, you're a young man. You can guess what else we might do. She's quite good."

Lan sampled the clearing for magics and found nothing but the overwhelming presence of the Pillar of Night. These stick and leaf dolls were not animated; they were exactly as they appeared.

"This is Rook, a doughty warrior and defender of my

empire while I explore afield." Terrill picked up a figurine with a caked mud head and brought it over to Lan. "Don't be afraid. Even though he looks fierce, Rook is quite gentle with people he knows."

An arm fell off. Terrill hastily glued it back on, spitting on dirt to soften it to sticky mud.

"Did Claybore do this?"

"What? On, no, not possible. Rook was injured in battle with a sixty-foot-long dragon. Killed it, he did. Fantastic battle. No, Claybore doesn't dare approach any of us. Rook can protect us. And if he can't, there are others." Terrill's voice dropped to a confidential whisper. "We are able to repel any invaders to our forest."

"The others I met in the forest," Lan asked. "What of them?"

"Other humans? All mages. All left here by Claybore. Ugly people. Rook keeps them away, don't you, Rook?" Terrill shook the doll so that it bobbed up and down in assent.

Lan turned cold inside. This haunted forest held the husks of sorcerers who had opposed Claybore. Something about the Pillar of Night held them within the forest, and Claybore's tender mercies had driven them insane before even coming here. Many Claybore had experimented on to find substitutes for his lost limbs and all he had tortured to insanity. What had he done to Terrill, his most successful adversary? Lan didn't want to know.

"Tell me of the Pillar," Lan asked.

"Nothing to tell. Claybore's supreme magic, and it failed. Oh, yes, it failed him at the last moment. Didn't drive home."

"What do you mean?"

"Would you stay for our feast? Rook has slain a fire elemental and three demons and my paramour is especially amorous tonight." Terrill gave Lan a lewd wink. "She has many ladies in waiting who would enjoy your company."

Lan looked at the stick figurines and shuddered. Terrill's power had fled with his sanity.

"How long have you been here?" Lan asked.

"Forever. Ten thousand years. Maybe more, maybe less. Who can say?"

"You are immortal?"

"That power remains," Terrill said wistfully. "But do come and sit down. Our feast is just beginning." Terrill started digging with his fingers in the soft dirt and produced a tuber. "More sumptuous than anything a king might dine upon!"

Lan waited until Terrill presented this fine viand to his champion, Rook. Then Lan slipped into the forest, repressing the urge to run until his feet wore down to his ankles. Out of sight of the demented sorcerer, Lan shook and felt hot tears of rage and frustration trickling down his cheeks. His hands clenched tightly and he wished for nothing more than the chance to slay Claybore.

He went to the edge of the forest again and peered at the blackness of the Pillar of Night. Gently, he sailed his light mote out to explore its vastness. The magical column tried to suck in his familiar, but Lan's power was great enough to prevent it; he knew that he would follow the dancing mote in if it were to succumb to the immense negative forces of the Pillar.

Lan Martak tried minor spells and scouted the base, never actually getting close enough to touch it physically. Tired and disheartened, he turned away and went back through the forest. He passed near Terrill's clearing. The once-great mage and his entourage were enjoying a millennia-long celebration.

"So this is what it means to live forever," Lan said. As silent as a shadow he moved on through the forest, stalked by trees and wounded by spined plants.

He did not rest until he came to the far edge of the forest, where he found his demon-powered flyer. The demon trapped within cursed volubly at his sorry fate.

Lan forced such exertion on the demon that, by the time they returned to Brinke's castle, the demon was too exhausted to do more than wheeze.

•   •   •

"You are certain it was Terrill?" the Lady Brinke asked. "I had never envisioned him in such straits. He was always bigger than life, a giant of magics. Long before I heard of Claybore I had heard the tales of Terrill's fine deeds, his philanthropy and kindness."

"Once, he might have been. Of all the humans I saw in Claybore's forest, Terill is the only one who retained all his bodily parts. Claybore either didn't or couldn't experiment on Terrill."

The tall blonde pulled a scarlet robe more tightly around her svelte body. "The power of the forest binds them, just as we are bound to Claybore."

"Terrill did say one thing which puzzles me. He . . ." Lan snapped his mouth closed when Kiska k'Adesina blasted into the room. She shook with fury.

"How *dare* you leave me like this?" she screamed. "For almost three weeks you left me. And she treated me like a prisoner. I won't stand for it. You love me, Lan, you know you do." Kiska went on, in a softer, more seductive voice. "Why punish me like this?"

Lan wanted to burn her to a cinder with a single quick spell. "I love you," he choked out. "I had to go and . . ."

"Lan," broke in Brinke. "We can discuss this later." Her almost colorless grey eyes warned him not to reveal too much to Kiska.

"Yes, later," agreed Kiska. "Lan and I need time to ourselves. For a proper welcoming home."

"No," Lan said weakly. But he allowed Kiska to lead him from the chamber and to their sleeping quarters. The more he fought the geas, the more certainly he fell under its power. He apologized to Kiska for leaving her and only through a phenomenal power of will kept from telling her where he had gone.

After they had made love, Lan lay staring at the stone wall. He thought of Terrill and the curse of immortality. The mage had attained such power that he could never die. But the quality of how he spent eternity mattered, Lan saw. Insane.

He left Kiska in the bed and softly padded across the

cold floor to find his clothing. He knew a fate worse than Terrill's: to be forced to spend all of time loving a woman he hated. Lan glanced at the sleeping Kiska k'Adesina and wished he had the skill to slip free of Claybore's geas. Otherwise he and Kiska might be together for a long, long time.

Brinke stared through the empty archway at the end of her chamber. From deep within she felt stirrings of magic. The woman coaxed them and guided the forces outward. Untutored though she was, Brinke managed to form a scrying spell of some power.

The Pillar of Night rose, sleek and black and devouring all light. She flinched at its sight and wondered why she had never sensed this potent structure's existence on her world before. Lan Martak's presence lent her courage. With him alongside, she dared to explore, to even think of defeating Claybore.

Her handling of the scrying spell became increasingly inadequate. The view wavered and finally fell apart in a chaos of colors. Brinke released the spell and sank forward, weakened by her effort.

"You do improve, though, dear Brinke," came a voice from behind her carved chair. The woman jerked around, startled.

"Claybore!"

"Always before you denied the Pillar's existence, as I intended. It amuses me to see you have overcome that portion of my geas. But I must save that for another visit. I've come to visit and to find what our mutual friend is up to."

The woman rose, her hand seeking out a silver dagger from its sheath under her scarlet robe. The slim blade flicked out and rammed straight for its target in Claybore's slightly protuberant belly. The sharp tip stopped a fraction of an inch away. Strain as she would, Brink couldn't finish the thrust.

"Must it always be this way?" Claybore asked peevishly. "I do wish you'd learn not to oppose me."

"What do you mean, 'always this way'?"

Claybore chuckled, his bone skull giving no indication of where the sound came from. Ruby whirlwinds spun in the dark eye sockets. Twin beams lashed out and pinioned Brinke. She stiffened, her eyes losing focus and her lovely face turning slack.

"Martak went to the Pillar of Night," said Claybore. "What did he learn there?"

"He has not said," Brinke reported.

"Does he suspect you?"

"No."

"Good. I loathe giving up one of my most useful spies. He has sensed the geas I have placed upon you?"

"Yes."

"But he hasn't learned it is a spell of control, that I only activate it to force you to speak of my enemies' plans?"

"No."

Claybore's mechanical legs carried him around. One hand lifted and stroked over Brinke's cheek. The woman did not respond.

"Soon enough all my parts will be in their proper place. Martak will be dead—or worse. I think he will make a fine companion for Terrill in my little forest preserve, don't you?" Claybore didn't expect an answer. "When I am again whole, you and I will spend much time together. Would you like that?"

"No!"

"You will like it," he said flatly. "The geas will insure that. What else have you learned of Martak's excursion?"

"Nothing."

"Very well. Learn what you can. And, as always, you will not remember talking to me or seeing me. My presence here will be permanently forgotten." Claybore manipulated the spell binding the woman, made certain forgetfulness was visited upon her, then left.

Brinke sagged, the silver dagger dropping from her hand. She stared at it, not remembering how it had come to hand or why she would have wanted to draw it. The headache building behind her eyes was worse than ever. Sprites kicked and tore at the backs of her eyeballs until she moaned aloud.

Brinke vowed to see the chirurgeon about a potion to alleviate it. The headaches were becoming more frequent.

She picked up her dagger and left the chamber, curiously drained of vitality.

Twin morning stars vied for supremacy in the east. Only faint pink fingers of dawn threatened them and set them adrift in a sky of grey. Lan Martak leaned over the castle battlements and watched as the pinks turned to light yellows and the sun poked a bright rim above the horizon. Chill breezes blew off the grain fields surrounding Brinke's castle and contrasted vividly with the sterility of Claybore's forest circling the Pillar of Night. Idly running his fingernails along rough stone, he traced out a map of all he saw before him—and placed the dark Pillar at the very edge.

Soft shuffling sounds brought him around.

"I couldn't sleep," said Brinke. "I often come up here to see the new day being born."

"I couldn't stand being with Kiska an instant longer," Lan said, knowing it was a lie even as he spoke the words. The geas forced him to seek out Claybore's commander, to want to be with her. Only an extreme effort of will allowed him to part from her. To be with her again had been one of the strongest needs driving him back from the Pillar.

"You look distracted," Brinke said. "Do you want to talk about it?"

Lan started to speak, then stopped. Something felt wrong, different. And it was with Brinke.

"What have you been doing?" he asked.

"I? Nothing. Well, I did attempt a scrying of the Pillar."

"There is more."

Brinke shook her head. She glanced away from Lan to the sunrise, then back. "This time of day is always a comfort. Quiet, serene, it makes me believe better times are possible for all of us."

"Claybore," Lan said, more to himself than to Brinke.

"Do not ruin the mood," she gently chided. "Just enjoy the glory of a day filled with bright promise."

"Claybore has done something to you. There is a residue lingering around you that carries his imprint. I know it well. I've fought it long enough."

"I don't know what you mean." Panic flared and died in the woman's eyes. This convinced Lan he had not been mistaken.

"You mentioned a geas upon you," Lan said. "I have never really felt it—not before this. What makes you think Claybore has done anything to you?"

"Why, I . . . I don't know. I can't say, but I know it is true."

Lan snorted in contempt. "Claybore plays with you. He has laid a compulsion of some sort on you and lets you know it, just as he does with me."

"But I feel no presence, as you do, Lan."

"I sense it." Lan closed his eyes and began to expand the light mote to a hollow sphere enclosing both him and Brinke. Lan had never attempted this before; he wanted to shield his activities from Claybore's prying eyes. Any blatant use of truly powerful magics would draw the sorcerer. Lan still needed to hide his actions until he had worked through the reason behind the Pillar of Night.

"What are you doing?" cried Brinke. The blonde tried to force her way through the shimmery curtain of light encapsulating them.

"Seeking out the root of your geas. If Claybore left you the knowledge that he had placed it upon you, there's a chance I can trace back along that path and find the exact spell."

"No, Lan, I'm not under any spell. Not now. No, oh, no!"

The tall woman slumped. Lan caught her and eased her to the stone battlements. The knowledge of the spell being placed flitted lightly across the surface of her being. Lan grabbed it forcefully and pulled. What he saw magically as a tiny thread ran down into the woman's very soul. He followed, probing carefully, placing ward spells at every stage to prevent Claybore from taking him by surprise.

The magical surgery resulted in excising a tiny, glowing knot from deep within Brinke's being. Lan plucked it forth and crushed it as he would a tick.

Lan released the shell around them. The entire countering had taken less than a minute.

"He visited me often!" gasped Brinke. "I remember now. He got information from me, then ordered me to forget. And I did. I was a traitor. I betrayed those best able to oppose Claybore and never knew it until this moment. And my sister. I betrayed her to him!" Brinke turned and stared into the sun. One slender foot went up to the crenelation. She hoisted herself up and looked out into the distance.

Lan didn't understand what she did until it was almost too late to act. He surged forward and grabbed a double handful of the thick robe just as Brinke jumped. The heavy fabric ripped but held well enough for him to pull her back to the battlements.

"Why did you do that?" He probed her for some lingering effect of the spell. Claybore was wily enough to plant a second compulsion spell to make her kill herself if found out.

"I betrayed my friends and family. I would have betrayed you, but I knew nothing of your trip."

"You didn't do this," Lan said quickly, trying to convince the woman. "Claybore is a mage of vast power. Your magics cannot stand against his. Don't surrender to him by killing yourself. Fight him! If you truly hate what he's made you do, fight him with all your strength. Don't give in to him."

Brinke swallowed hard and pulled free. Lan watched for a telltale sign that she might try suicide gain. The blonde leaned forward on the rough-hewn stone and bowed her head.

"You are right. But I feel so... used!"

"He is expert at manipulating people, with or without spells," said Lan. "Look how he uses me as a pawn. Kiska provides control over me, both day and night. Leaving her is a major act of courage on my part."

"But you do it."

"I must, but each time is more difficult. Claybore is evil

and brings stark horror wherever he goes." Lan thought of the forest again with its mutilated, insane inhabitants. Terrill, of all those poor wights, caused Lan to mourn the most. Terrill's fate would be his, if he failed.

Lan would not fail.

"The geas," said Brinke. "Do you think I might be able to help you break it? As you broke mine?"

"You have the power, but it is undisciplined," said Lan, considering it. "What have I to lose?"

"I might do something wrong and injure you."

Insanity. Living for all eternity a madman like Terrill. Lan forced the thoughts from his mind. Also pushed aside was the paranoid idea that Claybore engineered all this, that he wanted Brinke to attempt the spells and drive Lan crazy.

"Do it," he said. He let the light mote spread out and surround them once more to insure a modicum of privacy from Claybore's prying. Then Lan relaxed the impenetrable barriers within him that he had maintained for so long.

Feathery touches across the surface of his mind told him Brinke sought the geas. He stared off into the sunrise, the light hurting his eyes as he looked directly into the white-hot sun.

He winced, then pulled away, only to relax and allow Brinke another try. And another and still another. Finally the woman shook her head, blonde hair spilling forward and into her eyes. She pushed it back with a gesture showing her frustration.

"Lan, I'm sorry. I cannot do it. The geas is there. I *see* it magically. But I cannot alter it. The spells Claybore used are too strong."

"Too subtle," Lan corrected. "He has insinuated them into my mind and I can do nothing about it. Only my ability prevented him from planting a self-destructive compulsion."

"I tried, Lan," repeated Brinke. "I'm so sorry. I'm freed and you aren't."

Lan Martak knew she was not the only one who felt sorry.

CHAPTER ELEVEN

"Lan! I awoke and you were gone. Is anything wrong?" Kiska k'Adesina strutted onto the battlements, her garments only half fastened. Lan saw large expanses of bare skin gleaming in the morning light and began to respond to the erotic provocations.

The geas definitely had not been lifted from him.

"I'm not interrupting anything, am I?" asked Kiska. Coyness did not sit well with her. She was whipcord thin and lacked the stature to make such work to her benefit. But Lan hardly noticed. His body already responded to her overtures.

Brinke cleared her throat and said, "I'll be down in my chambers. I'll expect you at breakfast, Lan."

"Perhaps noon hour," cut in Kiska.

Brinke pulled her torn robes around her and walked off, regal and proud. Lan started to go with her, but Kiska's insistent fingers touched his cheek, his lips, his chest and lower. He gave in to the full power of Claybore's geas once again. He could do nothing else.

For the moment.

• • •

He had only a few minutes to speak with Brinke before Kiska came. He used the time to full advantage.

"Claybore learned nothing of my trip from you?" he asked.

"You told me little," the blonde responded.

"Good. That was fortuitous." Brinke blushed in embarrassment. Lan hastily said, "I meant nothing by it, only that we are in a stronger position now than before. Claybore might not know I spoke to Terrill."

"No, his question to me was about the Pillar of Night, not Terrill. I only answered direct questions and never volunteered information. I was that much in control, at least."

"Terrill told me that the Pillar was Claybore's finest spell, the one that almost allowed him total domination ten thousand years ago, but hinted that it failed in some respect. Do you know anything about it?"

"Little. Only recently have I found the proper scrying spells to even look at it," said Brinke. "But rumors, half truths, perhaps outright lies. Those I have heard. I know that Claybore wiped even the name from my memory, but he hardly needed to do so. Even before this geas, I knew nothing important."

Lan nodded for her to continue. Any conjecture, no matter how farfetched, might aid him now. He believed the demented mage when Terrill told him of failure. The titanic battle of magics so many thousands of years ago had not resulted in a clear-cut victor. Terrill still wandered about playing with his artificial friends and Claybore's bodily parts were only now being regained. Beyond this, Lan wondered if still another player in the drama wasn't of greater importance than he—seemed.

"What of the Resident of the Pit?" he asked Brinke.

"The Resident of the Pit?" she asked, startled. "I was about to mention this. One tale has it that Claybore imprisoned the Resident inside the Pillar of Night."

"He caged a god?"

Brinke shrugged shapely shoulders. "I cannot conceive

of such a thing, but you must be able to."

"Me?" laughed Lan. "Why me?"

The woman's face turned serious. "You are as much a god as Claybore."

"No!"

"You are," she insisted. "The powerful aura surrounding you also emanates from Claybore. But it is different in substance. You are less avaricious."

"That's all?" Lan didn't care for the comparison.

"Yes."

Had he become so like his enemy? Lan leaned back in his chair and munched at a juicy persimmon. He spat out the seeds and magically caught them in midair. So easy, he mused. The spells he had once commanded were minor healing spells and the ability to light a campfire by a spark from his fingertips, spells useful to a hunter. Now he summoned elementals, sent whirlwinds and fireballs against his enemies with the ease he used to draw a bow and loose an arrow. A pass of his hand and the proper chant might destroy not only this castle and everyone in it but the entire world.

His mind turned over and over the spell required to crack the planet open to its center.

It wasn't that difficult. Not for him. Not for a god.

Lan dropped the seeds to the table and straightened. He was not a god. He would not be a god, no matter how much the Resident of the Pit pushed him in that direction.

"It might be true," he said, "about the Resident being imprisoned in the Pillar of Night." Brinke noted his sudden change of topic. She made a great show of carefully slicing a freshly baked loaf of bread, her eyes avoiding his. "The Resident has aided me on occasion and I never decided why."

"He wants to be released?"

"He wants to die," Lan said. After meeting Terrill and seeing the mage's pathetic existence, he sympathized with the Resident, if the god were trapped within the Pillar.

Lan looked over his shoulder and asked, "I wonder what's keeping Kiska? She should have been here by now."

"Let her be," the blonde said. But Lan couldn't. He left to find Kiska.

Brinke chewed slowly at the slab of bread she'd cut. A presence in the room made her turn.

"Claybore!"

Standing by the door was the mage, his metal legs gleaming and one arm held in a sling. A ragged incision ran around the shoulder, showing where someone had tried to stitch the arm back and had failed.

"I need to know what Martak discovered at the Pillar of Night. Tell me!"

Brinke experienced waves of heat assaulting her. Sweat beaded on her brow, but she did not speak. The geas Claybore had laid upon her was truly gone.

"So he removed it," said Claybore. "Little matter. While I hate losing such a valued source of information, you are certainly the least of my informants."

"Liar. You had great need for me or you wouldn't have kept me as you did."

"Your beauty is great," Claybore said, "but do not substitute it for common sense. Why would I need you at all?"

"To use against Lan. You fear him. He controls powers great enough to destroy you."

"I am immortal," scoffed Claybore. "Since my geas has been lifted, I must apply a different spell. Time presses in on me. I must learn what Martak knows of the Pillar of Night. Tell me!"

Brinke let out a tiny gasp and rose from her chair. She staggered and fell heavily against the table, barely supporting herself. From all sides the very air crushed in upon her, draining her of strength, forcing her to speak.

"Tell me what I wish and you can be free of this torture."

"You'll kill me if I tell you."

"I'll find out, whether you are alive or dead. My power goes beyond the grave, my lovely Brinke. Tell me!"

"I refuse." She tried to scream as pain wracked her body. Brinke knew the sorcerer ripped off her arms and legs and pulled her head from her neck. Stark agony unlike anything she had ever experienced dazzled her senses and made her more and more compliant to Claybore's wishes. But she fought. From deep within herself she found reserves of strength and she fought.

"It will only take a bit more and you will die. Can such paltry information be worth this to you? Or do you enjoy pain?"

Claybore sent needles of anguish jabbing into her most private recesses. Brinke resisted, even though she weakened visibly. And then the pain evaporated.

"Martak!" shrieked the dismembered sorcerer.

"You forced only a spell of compulsion on her. I planted a few ward spells to aid her. She is no match for you. Shall we see who is the stronger, you or me?"

The spell Lan cast was both potent and subtle. He saw the way Claybore wore the sling to support the damaged arm. Like a buzz saw, Lan sent a plane of pure energy down against the shoulder joint. Claybore's arm fell away. Whatever misfortune had caused the arm to require support now aided Lan's attempt to dismember Claybore again.

Only the cloth sling supported the arm; Lan's spell had rived it cleanly.

Claybore tried to destroy Brinke, but Lan anticipated— and he had learned. Claybore's spell lacked full power. If the mage succeeded in killing Brinke, he would leave himself open to Lan's counterattack. Already Claybore's other arm twitched and jerked with a life of its own as it tried to slip from the shoulder joint.

Claybore had the same choice he had given Lan earlier. He might slay Brinke, but he would lose at least his arms and possibly more.

"Your fate will be excruciating, Martak," raged Claybore. The sorcerer vanished from the chamber.

Lan's eyebrows rose. He analyzed the spell Claybore had used—it was identical to the one he had pioneered for movement between worlds without the use of a cenotaph.

"He's stolen it from me," Lan said aloud. He didn't know if he ought to be pleased at the theft or not. Claybore's

comings and goings had been limited when Lan ripped out
the Kinetic Sphere and cast it at random along the Road.
Now that Claybore employed the same movement spell he
did, Lan no longer had the advantage of mobility over his
foe.

"You saved me," sobbed out Brinke. She threw her arms
around his neck and buried her face in his shoulder. He felt
the wetness of her tears dampening his tunic. "I told him
nothing. I resisted."

"I know," said Lan, renewed by the feel of Brinke's
sleek body in his arms. "Your powers may be untutored,
but they are greater than either of us thought. You did not
give in to him and Claybore used potent spells against you."

"Your ward spells helped."

Lan laughed. "There were no ward spells. Oh, I used
them when initially finding the geas within your mind, but
I didn't want to impose my spells on you. You were free
of them—and you kept Claybore away through your own
efforts."

Brinke said nothing, a shy smile crossing her lips. The
smile vanished when Kiska came barreling into the room.

"So here you are. Why is it I always find the pair of you
together?" Her tone was intended to cut deeply. And it did.
Lan had to bite back an apology.

"It is nothing," he said. "We were merely discussing
how best to defeat Claybore."

"If you want to defeat him," said Kiska in a confidential
tone, "you'll forget all about this Pillar of Night."

"What?" This took Lan unexpectedly.

"The Pillar of Night. You mentioned it many times.
Remember, my darling? Or has this . . . lovely woman
addled your senses?"

"I remember. What do you mean, I should avoid it?"

"The fine lady doesn't know this," said Kiska, "but the
Pillar is still another of Claybore's pieces."

Brinke laughed at this. "No one is so well endowed."

"Slut," snapped Kiska. "In the strictest sense, it is not a
part of his body. Rather, it is more. Far more."

"He has his arms back," said Lan. He had to silently congratulate himself on the devastation he had wrought on Claybore's limbs. "His heart has been sent skittering along the Road to who knows where. I still possess his tongue and the facial skin has been destroyed. We know torso and skull are still joined and the legs are gone. What's left?"

Kiska looked from one to the other, a serious expression settling over her. "His very soul, that's what."

"Claybore has no soul," scoffed Brinke.

"That is true—now. But Terrill wrenched it free from him and imprisoned it inside the Pillar of Night. If you unbalance the delicate spells surrounding the Pillar, Claybore will regain a vital portion of his whole. It might even be the most significant portion."

"She lies, Lan," Brinke said with some asperity. "She only seeks to have you divert your energies elsewhere and allow Claybore to do his evil deeds unopposed."

"How would the blonde bitch know anything? Claybore uses her. In all ways." The sneer twisting Kiska's lips cut deeply into Lan. He was torn between the two women. He believed Brinke's story of the Pillar of Night rather than Kiska's. It explained all the details and contradicted none of the facts.

But he loved Kiska. He had to listen to her wild rantings, even though he knew she probably lied. Or did she? Claybore played a complex game that confused Lan more and more. The other sorcerer was not content with only dealing lies. He delved into the realm of half truths and even cunningly told truths that sounded as if they might be lies.

Frustration rose in Lan. Since Inyx and Krek had left him, he had nowhere to turn for aid. Or even comfort. Brinke was lovely and adept enough with simple magics, but she was not Inyx.

Kiska? If he could, he would kill her. Instead, he took the woman in his arms and kissed her.

"I love you," he said. "But this story—this fable—cannot be true."

"But it is!" Kiska protested.

"I have spoken with Terrill," he said.

"Lan!" Brinke's eyes widened in horror at what the mage said. But Lan found himself unable to stop now that he'd begun. The geas wormed words from his lips that he had not meant to utter.

But this was Kiska k'Adesina, the woman he loved. He had to reveal this to her, even as he felt the spell working within his mind like a worm burrowing through the earth. Its power expanded and his own control diminished.

"Tell me about it," urged Kiska.

"Terrill did not say anything about its being Claybore trapped within the Pillar. Indeed, he hinted that there is nothing *within* but rather under."

"That Terrill stays near the Pillar of Night is proof enough that she lies, Lan. Do not listen to her." Brinke pleaded with him now, but Lan fell increasingly under the power of the geas, in matters both physical and emotional.

"So you talked to Terrill at the base of the Pillar?" Kiska smiled slyly.

Lan's mind turned to the possibility that Kiska spoke the truth. Terrill might have been driven insane by the power of his own spell. When learning the more complex incantations, Lan himself had teetered on the edge of losing control and being destroyed. With a potent construct like the Pillar of Night, he couldn't say what forces had been summoned to create it.

"Claybore's soul," he mused.

"Yes!"

"No!" protested Brinke. "Listen to her and you will never defeat Claybore."

"If I shatter the spells holding the Pillar together, I might play into Claybore's hands."

"His severed hands," said Brinke. "Remember what you did to him just a short while ago. He cannot hold himself together. He already nears the limits of his power. Release that held prisoner by the Pillar of Night and Claybore will fall victim to you in short order."

"He was here?" cried Kiska. "Claybore?"

Lan's head began to hurt. He found it harder to concentrate and soon conjured a small spell to shut out all sound. He let the women argue while he sat in a magically induced silence.

"Inyx," he said softly. "I need you. You always saw so clearly. Even you, Krek. Even you, I need now."

He released the spell and tried to follow the ebb and flow of the argument between Brinke and Kiska. Nothing was settled. He would have to decide which of them spoke truly.

Which one?

Act against the Pillar of Night and release a god—the Resident of the Pit? Or act against it and release the single most vital portion contributing to Claybore's power? Or do nothing?

Lan Martak had no answer.

CHAPTER TWELVE

Claybore swiveled about on his mechanical hips as he studied the softly glowing wall. If his fleshless skull had possessed lips, he would have smiled in satisfaction. As it was, the white bone took on a higher sheen and a tiny crack began to run from one eye socket up to the crown. Claybore didn't notice. His full attention focused on the wall and the scenes beginning to appear.

"Good," he said to his assistant mage. "You have done well, Patriccan."

Patriccan hobbled over and propped himself against a table littered with charts, grimoires, and other magical paraphernalia. He, too, rejoiced in all that transpired on a dozen different worlds.

"Master, your scrying improves. None sees onto another world along the Road save you. And now you are able to maintain viewing ports to a full twelve worlds. Remarkable. I salute you." Patriccan bowed as deeply as he could. His injuries had still not healed, even though he had ordered several of his junior sorcerers to use what healing spells they knew. It had come as a shock to Patriccan to find they knew very few—their expertise, like his own, lay in the field of destruction, not healing.

Claybore strutted back and forth like a partly mechanical, partly flesh, partly decayed rooster. From the pits of his eye sockets came a directing beam of pale red. The beams struck a spot on the wall and created a picture different only in detail. Like the others, this one also showed carnage and suffering.

"You have recovered the Kinetic Sphere for me?" Claybore asked. "I see my agents with it on this world."

"Martak failed to hide it properly, master," said Patriccan. The mage shifted his weight and forced away the pain he experienced. If he could not take full revenge on Inyx, Ducasien and the others on that backwater world, he would at least revel in his master's scheme to humiliate and destroy Martak.

"He did not try. It came as a surprise to him that he was able to yank it from my chest." A hesitant hand touched the putresence around the gaping hole in Claybore's chest. The hand shook uncontrollably; the arm had not been properly restored. New spells were required for permanent attachment.

"Look, master," said Patriccan. "Our legions conquer still another world. Their king bows his knee to your supreme rule."

"Pah," snorted Claybore. "Who cares for petty rulers? Or even if they are led by mages of some power. They are ants. So what if it is an entire world coming under my aegis? The real battle continues here and here and . . . here."

He pointed to scenes from the world where Ducasien and Inyx consolidated their power, to a scene with Brinke and Lan Martak and to the darkly towering Pillar of Night.

"Master, rest assured all will be ready when the final battle trumpet is sounded."

"Don't be so dramatic, Patriccan. It ill becomes you. This will be a bloody fight, a good one. I relish the thought of Martak squirming, begging me for mercy."

"He proved incapable of defending himself," Patriccan

said ingratiatingly, "because of your cunning geas."

"I worry about that," admitted Claybore. The death's head craned about and faced Patriccan. "He is more powerful than I in some respects and knows how that compulsion wears down on his ability. If Kiska is somehow killed, he would be forced to mourn, but my control over him would be gone."

"He cannot allow that."

"And I work constantly to be sure she is not placed in jeopardy, but his friends"—Claybore tapped the glowing screen where Inyx and Ducasien toiled—"are not without their own quaint powers. They might eliminate Kiska before I can play her in the proper sequence."

"You will let her slay Martak?" Patriccan's surprise was real. Martak had proved Claybore's most able rival since Terrill. To allow another, a mere soldier, to kill Martak struck the mage as sacrilege. "I will perform the task for you. I have no love of him, either. Do not let her simply drive a dagger into his back."

"Why not? What worse fate for someone such as he? To be killed by the one you love."

"He is being forced."

"It won't matter. But you are wasting precious time. Have you been successful in your experiments? I need complete outfitting before any major demands are placed on me."

"Master," Patriccan said, bowing again, "all is in readiness. Careful research has shown me the way to pioneer new spells that will prevent the rejection of your arms."

"Yes, yes," Claybore said impatiently. "I know all about that. My legs. What about my legs?"

The sorcerer's legs had been hacked apart and magically destroyed by Lan and were forever lost. Some time prior, Claybore had set Patriccan to preparing new legs.

"These may not provide the reservoir for the powers of your original limbs," said the journeyman mage, "but, master, they will suffice until better ones can be fashioned."

"Any of flesh and bone will be better than these me-

chanical atrocities." Claybore flexed one knee joint. It whined
in unoiled protest. The dancing spots of energy powering
the legs frequently winked out of existence and left the mage
motionless. "If you had not perfected the organic limbs, I
would have considered conjuring a minor demon to provide
the motive power."

Patriccan shook his head at this. Even the most minor
of demons were cantankerous and turned on both mortal
and mage with—demonic—glee. To rely on one was sheer
folly, even when the binding spells were as potent as the
ones Claybore might conjure.

"The legs await you, master."

Patriccan hobbled ahead of Claybore. The mage went
into his laboratory and waved away his numerous assistants.
Many were young and barely trained, while others were
almost as experienced as Patriccan. Whether apprentice or
journeyman mage, they all paid obeisance to Claybore. They
knew the penalty for not doing so.

The mutilated husks of mages who had opposed Claybore
littered the haunted forests surrounding the Pillar of Night.
None wished to spend the rest of eternity sightless, insane,
without the proper number of limbs and organs.

"Remarkably similar to my own," said Claybore, standing at the edge of a green-tiled table. Human-appearing legs
twitched feebly on the slick surface. Two mages sat on the
far side of the table, eyes closed to enhance concentration,
their lips moving constantly in the spells required to keep
the legs alive until attached to their master.

Claybore made several passes with his hands over the
juncture between machine and flesh. A hissing noise caused
several of the mages to recoil. Smoke rose from the metal
legs and momentarily obscured the dismembered sorcerer.
As the smoke blew away all that remained was a molten
puddle of metal on the floor. Claybore hovered in midair.

"This taxes me more than I thought, Patriccan. Hurry."

"Rest on the table, master. Would you prefer a soporific
spell?"

"No! I stay aware of all that happens."

Patriccan acquiesced to the desire. It did not pay to make Claybore angry or upset. Patriccan motioned to those chanting the preservation spells. They backed off, their chants dropping in volume until they were barely audible.

Others moved closer, bringing with them special pastes and magically enhanced sections of living flesh. Patriccan personally placed the left leg into the raw hip socket. Sweat broke out on his forehead and ran into his eyes as the strain mounted. He blinked it free as he worked, not daring to take his hands away from the task. The paste smeared over the end of the leg allowed a perfect junction to be made. Rapid, complex spells bonded flesh to flesh.

"There is no feeling in the leg. It is dead," said Claybore. His peevish tone spurred Patriccan and the others to greater effort. The leg began twitching spastically. "There," said Claybore with some satisfaction. "I can even wiggle the toes. It is good."

"The other leg," muttered Patriccan. "Hurry with it. Hurry!" The other mages slid it along the green tile. Patriccan applied the pastes and chanted the spells.

Try as he would, he failed to make the proper connections. Nerve endings refused to weld and the leg began withering.

"Do not let it die," warned Claybore. "One leg avails me little. I must have both."

"Master, there is only one way to salvage this leg. Something has gone wrong. The flesh was not properly activated. I . . . I do not know what to do, other than to summon a demon."

"Do it." Claybore's words were cold, unemotional. He and Patriccan both knew the penalty for failure. Claybore was immortal and could not die, but eternity spent in a burned or mutilated state was an eternity of damnation.

Two of the less brave mages slipped from the chamber, faces white and teeth chattering with fear. Patriccan found himself in little better condition, but knew what had to be done.

He made the hand gestures in the air and traced out fiery

trails of incandescent green and purple. The spell wove into a complex melange of syllables hardly intelligible. The very air of the room began to hum and churn with the power of the conjuring. The demon puffed into existence, sending fly ash and sparks outward in a small cloud.

"Obey," Patriccan said. His fingers forged a cage with bars of glowing colors; the demon struggled against the imprisoning bars. One taloned hand snaked between two bars that had been carelessly constructed and a long nail scratched down the side of Patriccan's face. The sorcerer jerked back, anger flaring. He pointed, the tip of his finger turning white-hot. He started to send the demon back to the netherworld from which it had been summoned.

"No," said Claybore. "Proceed. Use this one."

"A sorry wreck you are," observed the demon. "Not even I can piece you back together, even if I wanted. And I don't." The demon sat cross-legged within the cage and licked Patriccan's blood from its talon. It made a face and spat. The gobbet struck one bar and sizzled.

Only with extreme effort did Patriccan control himself. Claybore desired a quick end to this. To conjure another demon might take more time and energy than he had. Patriccan moved the bars closer together to prevent another attempt at injuring him.

"Animate the leg. Give it the essence that burns within your veins. Give it life!" Patriccan clapped his hands and pointed. The cage edged toward Claybore's leg. The demon tried to appear nonchalant but the spells holding it were strong. Reluctantly, the fierce green demon reached out and lightly touched Claybore's leg.

The shriek of agony filling the chamber had not been formed by human lips. New and deeper cracks appeared in Claybore's skull as the sorcerer endured the full anguish being meted out to him by the vindictive demon. Two of the braver mages near the back of the chamber whispered between themselves and then fell silent. Another wordless cry of pain lanced into their minds.

"He tortures me needlessly," shrieked Claybore. "I will

send him to the lowest of the Lowest Places for this. Oh, the pain, the pain! It must cease!"

Claybore thrashed about on the tiled table, hands gripping the edges for support. One arm began detaching at the shoulder; the mage found no strength within to perform the proper spell to keep it in place. Too many eons had passed since he had walked as a whole being. The parts had taken on auras of their own, grown in ways different from the torso. Claybore would have to force the arms back into place—later.

Now the mage had all he could contend with as the demon drew still another ideogram on his flesh and visited him with agony surpassing that ever borne by a living being.

"Mend the leg," ordered Patriccan. "Do it. *Do it!*"

"Oh, very well. There. It is done. Poor material I had to work with, though. Damn poor."

"I am a god," came Claybore's cold words. "You will rue the day you insulted me."

"They're all gods, to hear them talk," muttered the demon. He crossed his legs in the other direction and polished the long talons gleaming darkly.

"Your leg, master. Is it all right?" Patriccan asked anxiously.

"It is crooked." Claybore awkwardly slid off the table and stood on his legs. The one attached by the demon was inches shorter and bowed outward.

"Shoddy material, as I said," spoke up the demon.

"Shoddy workmanship," said Claybore. He placed his hands against the blazing bars of the cage and began squeezing. At first the demon only leered. Then it began to show more agitation as the bars closed in on it. Claybore continued to squeeze and the cage became ever smaller.

"Wait, stop. Don't!" the demon pleaded. "Perhaps I erred. Your legs are the finest I have ever seen."

Claybore's anger was not to be contained. He continued squeezing. The cage collapsed until the demon was held in a space less than an inch across. The keenings of outrage and fear filling the room now came solely from the demon.

"You thought I jested when I said I was a god. Know this, lowborn one. I am Claybore. I rule every world along the Road. And I rule you. You!"

"Y-yes, master," squawked the demon. "I see that now. Oh, the bars. They cut into me so cruelly! I hurt!"

"You'll hurt for a thousand years." Claybore conjured the world-shifting spell and exiled the demon to a distant place far from any civilized life.

"Is it cold there, master?" asked Patriccan.

"Very cold. The demon's punishment will be extreme." Patriccan bowed low, smiling.

"And the punishment of the two who spoke, saying I deserved such torture. . . ." Claybore hobbled about and directly faced the two miscreants. They dropped to their knees, pleading. From deep within Claybore's eye sockets boiled the ruby death beams. Both mages died in fierce convulsions, their bones breaking and their inner organs rupturing in the process.

"The Kinetic Sphere?" asked Claybore. "I want it now. With it I shall again be whole."

The parody of a human hobbled to where Patriccan opened a small cabinet. Inside lay the pinkly pulsing Kinetic Sphere, the sorcerer's heart. His shaky hands reached out and lifted it to the yawning cavity in his chest. Claybore thrust it into his body.

"The power again flows within me," he said. "I shall take a short rest to examine the additional powers that again having legs gives. Then," the mage said, fleshless skull catching the light and reflecting it whitely, "then Martak shall perish."

"Hail, master," cried Patriccan.

Claybore almost fell as he spun about, his bandy leg betraying him. With as much haughtiness as he could muster, the re-formed sorcerer strode from the room. Only when he reached the hall did he tend to his left arm, which had again fallen from his shoulder.

He was not as powerful as he had been before Terrill had dismembered him with the help of the Resident of the

Pit, but Claybore knew he was strong enough. For Inyx and Krek and Brinke and even Lan Martak.

"What is he doing?" Lan Martak worried at the lack of contact. "We cannot make the scrying spell work. He must be maneuvering into a position of power."

"My couriers report at least four worlds along the Road where his grey-clad legions have made their final bids for power—and have succeeded." Brinke stared at Lan, worry etched onto her fine face. "Physical power means little. He must seek other items, other powers, on those worlds."

Lan rubbed his tongue against dry lips. The metallic tang of that tongue reminded him of the energy and driving spells locked in each of Claybore's parts.

"He must have been prodigiously powerful when he met Terrill," Lan said. Fear began gnawing away at his confidence. He had been so certain that he and only he could defeat Claybore. Now he doubted himself. Had he the training, the power? What of experience? Claybore had tens of thousands of years of cunning to draw upon. Lan had succeeded this far only because the sorcerer had still been disassembled and strewn along the Road.

No longer was that an advantage. Lan tried to be realistic about Claybore's enhanced abilities—he assumed the sorcerer had regained the Kinetic Sphere. Lan had hardly known what he did when he ripped it from Claybore's chest. Even less did he know where he cast it. There had been no planning such as that Terrill employed when originally scattering Claybore's parts.

"The Pillar," said Lan. "The secret is there. If I only had some inkling as to what it was."

"No, Lan my darling," said Kiska, grabbing his arm and tugging hard. "You cannot return there. The spell holds Claybore's soul. He will become invincible if you meddle."

The woman's words started a different chain of thought. Lan said, "You argue for Claybore. He doesn't want me going to the Pillar because of what I might find."

"I have only your welfare at heart, Lan," Kiska said.

Brinke laughed derisively but Lan almost believed. He *loved* her, even as he saw the lies she told him. The geas chewed away at him and made him less than a man. He feared now, as much for Kiska's safety as his own. This robbed him of decisiveness.

Hands shaking and face pale with strain, he said, "I go back to the Pillar of Night. I must, if I am to discover the truth." He expected the Resident of the Pit to quietly concur. No phantom voice sounded within his head. He had made the decision. Now he had to act upon it.

"I'll go with you, Lan," said Brinke. "We . . . we make a good team." She flushed and smiled almost shyly.

"Bitch," snarled Kiska. "You lead him astray. Claybore will strip the flesh from his bones and fry him throughout all eternity for this. I love him!"

Lan prevented Brinke from using her silver dagger on Kiska. The blonde relented and said, "We must hurry, Lan. Claybore uses his time well. We know that from our inability to use the scrying spell. Before he is ready to attack, you must launch yours."

Lan nodded. He thought about the long journey using the demon-powered flyer. That had hidden any slight uses of magic he had performed, but the luxuries of time and seclusion were no longer his.

"We go. Now."

His dancing light mote swung in crazy orbits about his head. With a few simple spells, he elongated the dot of light until it once more encapsulated him and Brinke.

"Lan, you can't leave me!" pleaded Kiska, trapped outside the sphere of magic. "I need you!"

"She is a dagger at your throat, Lan. Leave her," urged Brinke.

"I . . ." Lan made an impatient gesture and breached the bubble so that Kiska could join them. She shot Brinke a look of pure venom as she rubbed seductively against Lan. The mage tried to ignore her and failed.

Magical bubble again intact, he used his transport spell to whisk them half a world away to the edge of the forest.

The bubble popped audibly and sent the trio tumbling to the ground.

"We are on the wrong side," said Brinke. "The Pillar is on the far side." She canted her head upward, trying to catch sight of the towering column of black.

"There is something about the forest that prevents you from seeing the Pillar," said Lan. "A few miles away, out on the plains, it is visible, immense, awesome. Move closer to the periphery of the forest and it vanishes."

"We walk?" asked Kiska. "I do not like this. Let's return to her castle, Lan. You can prepare for any battle there."

Lan did not answer. Swallowing the words of agreement, he walked briskly into the dead forest. Again he was struck by the deathly silence, the lack of bugs, the sterile odor, the sight of stalking plants and trees intent on encircling and killing.

The journey was rapid and without mishap. Before, Lan had hesitated to use his spells for fear of alerting Claybore. Now he felt time more precious than secrecy. The climactic battle neared with appalling rapidity, and Lan had to be armed with all the knowledge possible concerning the Pillar.

"You've returned, young man. How good of you to come see me," said the white-haired mage emerging from a clump of bushes. "But you were naughty. You ran off before we had our celebration. Rook hunted high and low for you and—but you have friends. How nice. You brought them for our party. Welcome," sad Terrill.

"His eyes," whispered Brinke. "Look at them."

"Life burns but no intelligence shines with it," agreed Lan. "This might be Claybore's ultimate torture."

"Keep this fool away from me," said Kiska.

"Terrill," said Lan, putting an arm around the ancient mage's shoulder and leading him away. "A word with you."

The man smiled at being taken into Lan's confidence.

"We are here in all secrecy—to visit the Pillar of Night. Can you aid us on this mission? Claybore must never know."

"Claybore?" he asked, voice quavering. "He sees all that happens within this forest. I invited him to one of our celebrations, but he never came. Rook felt very bad. So did Mela and Pekulline. They sulked for days."

"The Pillar," Lan pressed. "I would see it again. How do I get close?"

"He failed with it, Claybore did," said Terrill. "He only pinioned and did not skewer. Join us for our banquet this evening? We have many fine courses prepared." Terrill clutched another dirty tuber in his hands. Lan knew what the entree would be and sadly shook his head.

"No? Perhaps again, some other time." Terrill left without another word.

Lan rejoined Brinke and Kiska. The women were ready to come to blows when he stepped between them.

"Whatever the Pillar is, Terrill does not think it is Claybore's supreme achievement. Claybore failed with it."

"Yu would believe a demented old man?" Kiska crossed her arms and glared at both Lan and Brinke.

"We must hurry, Lan. I sense movement nearby." The lovely blonde gestured toward trees already sneaking up on them.

"Claybore must not stop me now. I must get closer to the Pillar." They started off at a trot, Kiska complaining with every step and Brinke struggling to keep up. When the magical pressures again shoved against Lan, he stopped.

"The Pillar of Night," he said.

"I see it. Through the trees. Just a bit," said Brinke, almost in awe. "It feels so . . . cold."

Lan closed his eyes and allowed his inner sense to guide him. The force against him mounted but he countered it. Closer he went to the intense black shaft. But he felt himself weakening. The powers locked within this tower of light-sucking darkness far transcended his own. He could not even conceive of the spell, the energy, the ability required to conjure such a permanent, potent monument.

A permanent, potent tombstone.

"I will aid you, Lan Martak," came a soft voice.

"Resident!"

"Closer. Come closer. I will it."

Lan took one hesitant step after another. The line of trees marking the ring of forest passed behind him. Only level, gravelly plain stretched up to the Pillar of Night. A hundred yards. Less. Fifty. He felt himself melting inside, merging with the Resident of the Pit. Twenty. Heat. He ignored it. Ten. Polar cold so intense his eyebrows froze. Five.

He reached out and placed his trembling hand against the Pillar of Night.

And Lan Martak knew. He knew the plight of the Resident of the Pit. He knew the mistakes Claybore had made fashioning the Pillar. Worst of all, he knew that, by himself, he would never be able to counter the spell holding the Pillar of Night in place.

CHAPTER THIRTEEN

"Go quickly. I do not think I can hold her long," said Brinke. She glanced nervously toward the room where Kiska lay trussed up and gagged. If the woman managed to work her way free and call out, Brinke and Lan both knew he would be unable to resist her pleas.

"I hate leaving . . . you," Lan said.

Brinke smiled wanly. "I know. And I know how difficult this is for you. The geas must be incredibly strong by this time." She lightly touched his cheek. "The geas laid upon me by Claybore was so much more than I could cope with. I know what you are going through."

Lan's heart beat rapidly. He closed his eyes and began the spell that would transport him across worlds in the span of a single heartbeat. If he lingered even a few minutes more, he ran the risk of being unable to leave at all without Kiska k'Adesina. His mission was such that he needed secrecy—and with her along to report directly to Claybore, despite his best efforts, he would fail.

"Hurry," he heard Brinke saying. The word lowered in pitch and the syllables drew out as he passed from one world to the next. When Lan blinked and peered about, he saw a rocky, barren world. A narrow canyon led into the higher mountains; the sheer cliff sides attracted his attention. Spider webs of enormous proportions depended from every outjut of rock and convenient spire.

"Krek," he said softly. "You have worked well here."

Lan started hiking, more for the sheer physical thrill than for any other reason. He had not refined the transport spell enough to pinpoint his destination, but he knew he could eliminate an hour or more of hard climbing by simple, short hops.

Lan Martak needed the exercise more than he needed to hurry. His life had been sedentary compared with the days of roaming the forests and living by his wits. Different skills had been sharpened, but at the expense of his strong sword arm, his indefatigable legs, his innate stamina. Also, this small hike gave him the opportunity to think of all that had occurred.

Touching the Pillar of Night had given him the truth. Kiska had lied; not something he had really doubted. And Brinke's retelling of the legends surrounding the Pillar had been incomplete. Claybore had trapped the Resident of the Pit—therein lay the mistake made by the sorcerer.

He had intended for the powerful spell to form the Pillar of Night and drive it directly through the core of the Resident of the Pit's being, killing the god for once and all time. The spell had failed at the last possible instant and had only trapped the god. Robbed of most of his power, the Resident had merely existed for the past ten thousand years with the Pillar as a tombstone to remind him of his former glory. Over this time he had come to long for death, even wishing Claybore had been successful with the original spell.

Lan could not defeat Claybore alone. He had fought to too many deadlocks to believe that now. His pride and overweening ego had been crushed by failure and forced him to admit he needed help.

He shook his head sadly. Together with the Resident of the Pit, he could defeat Claybore. To release the Resident from the Pillar of Night he needed the aid of others. He exhaled heavily when he realized that the friends he needed most were the very ones he had driven away.

Krek. Inyx. With their help he could free the Resident. With the Resident's help he could defeat Claybore.

Lan huffed and puffed up a final ridge and looked down the narrow alley shadowed by spider webs. No stream flowed but large, verdant spots showed that water seeped up from below. An underground river, perhaps. Perfect for a spider who hated water and yet depended on the bugs nourished on and in it.

The man squinted into the sunlight and saw tiny shapes moving along the walking strands of the web. The pattern was unfamiliar to Lan, but he decided Krek had been improvising, trying to nurture his artistic talents now that he had nothing else to do.

"Krek!" he called. "It's me, Lan Martak. Can we talk?"

Echoes reverberated down the valley. The tiny shapes in the web stopped and began swaying to and fro. The vibrations passed along certain cables in the web. Lan knew these spiders communicated with others, probably with Krek himself.

Lan trooped along, hunting for a small spring from which to slake his thirst. He found a bubbling pool and drank deeply from it, then sat and waited. Those spiders had sighted him and communication in the web was rapid and exact.

A spot twice as large appeared on the web and paused near the other two spiders. With long, loping steps, the distant spider dropped down to the bottom of the web and then to the ground out of Lan's sight. In less than five minutes Krek loomed above him, his coppery furred legs gleaming in the sun.

"Thank you for seeing me," Lan said.

Krek waited a spiderish length of time, then said, "Klawn always properly berated me for being brain-damaged. I know she is correct in that. Why I should desire to see you is beyond even my feeble power to imagine."

"I need your help, Krek. To free the Resident of the Pit, I need you."

"You are a powerful mage. Why do you need a craven one such as myself? You said as much before."

"I was wrong. I . . . I can't put into words what power you give me. It's true I am magically powerful. But I need more. Together, with you beside me, I can succeed. I apologize for any hurt. It's not much, but it's all I can offer at the moment."

"Contriteness does not suit you, Lan Martak." The spider folded his eight long legs and sank down slowly so that his large dun-colored eyes were level with Lan's. "I really ought to eat you for all you have done to me."

"I won't deny it." Lan carefully watched as the spider's huge mandibles clacked open and shut. One snip from those death scythes would end his life. Lan pulled his shoulders back and waited, wondering if Krek might attempt to cut him in half—and if both halves would continue to live. The magics within him were so potent, immortality might extend to even his pieces, just as it did to Claybore's. The thought of Claybore's mutilated foes scrabbling through the forest surrounding the Pillar of Night did not make him feel any better. Krek could doom him to such a fate with little effort.

"If I kill you, may I also eat you?"

"If you kill me, it won't much matter," said Lan.

The mountain arachnid thought on this for some time. Lan read not a hint of emotion in the chocolate pools of Krek's eyes. Only a soft breeze wafting through the valley disturbed the fur on his legs. Other than this slight movement, the giant spider might have been a rock.

"Humans taste funny," Krek finally said.

Lan did not answer. He interpreted this to mean Krek wasn't likely to eat him. But it was difficult to say.

"Come along. Let me show you my kingdom." Krek's long legs levered him upright again. With a dexterity that always amazed Lan, the spider pivoted and got all eight legs moving in ground-devouring moves.

Lan trailed behind, up a small, rocky path and into a

cave. He noticed Krek's reluctance to enter such a confined space but said nothing. Lan depended on Krek's good will now. Whatever the spider wanted to show him was fine, if it led to renewing their friendship.

"The mere spiders lost their Webmaster to the grey-clad humans," explained Krek as he lumbered along the low-ceilinged mineshaft. "I came along in time to show them how to defeat Claybore's soldiers. I am now Webmaster for the entire range, some forty thousand square miles of terrain."

"Congratulations," said Lan. "You were born to be a ruler."

"I often wonder," said Krek, sighing like a volcanic fumarole. "The demands are so wearing on me. It seems they never do things right the first time and I have to oversee their every web spin, their every hunting excursion."

They entered an immense chamber strung with webs on all walls and ceilings. On the floor lay skins similar to those shed by a snake, but their shape disturbed Lan.

Krek saw the man's interest.

"Claybore's soldiers," Krek explained.

"You ate them?"

"Not I personally. The mere spiders act like lowborns, at times. I try to elevate them to higher levels of sophistication and taste, but they resist. Another failure on my part, I fear. Sometimes I can be so inadequate, even in things I do well."

"But how?" asked Lan, looking at the fallen soldiers.

"We mountain arachnids have a somewhat different digestive process. We can rip off chunks of flesh and devour it." Krek's mandibles clanked shut to emphasize the process. "But the mere spiders only spit out a fluid, which dissolves the innards. They can then drink their prey. It is time-consuming because the acid works slowly, but it serves them well enough, I suppose." The spider shrugged it off, but Lan couldn't keep from staring at the husks of those who had once been humans.

"Is this what you wanted me to see?" Lan asked.

"What? The debris from sloppy eating? Hardly, Lan Martak. I have had ample time to work on my web. All Webmasters are entitled to perform one artistic masterwork for the edification of their underlings. This is mine."

Proudly, the spider lifted a middle leg and pointed.

"Krek, it's gorgeous," Lan said in true admiration. The other webs in the room were not spun by Krek, of that Lan had been certain the instant he spied them. They had been too small and lacked geometric complexity. But this web!

His eyes followed glistening strands and became confused by the profusion of color and cross-webbing. Sparkling diamonds and rubies glinted from strategic intersections and opalescent gems warmly accentuated the hard glitter of the other jewels. The strands themselves were of a kind Lan had not seen before. All the colors of the rainbow had been interwoven.

"In daylight, this would be an extraordinary work, Krek. Why did you hide it away in the cave?"

"One never boasts of one's web treasure," Krek said. "It might make the other spiders feel inferior, as they should in the presence of such grandeur."

"You are happy ruling here?"

"Passably so," said Krek, but Lan detected the faint tremors that indicated the spider meant more than he said.

Lan waited, saying nothing. Eventually Krek would elaborate. And he did.

"There is nothing to challenge me now that I have woven this web. How can anyone, even a Webmaster such as myself, improve upon perfection?"

"Would be hard," Lan agreed.

"With the grey-clads all removed and properly eaten, no danger looms to menace my web. Our hunting webs are adequate for years of sustained growth from our hatchlings. And they even seem to lack ambition."

"'They,' Krek?" Lan asked. "You talk of the mere spiders as if you were not one of them."

"Of course I am not one of them, you silly human. I am twice their size. More."

"You're their leader, their Webmaster."

"Such a burden it is, too." Krek sighed.

"There were fine times when we walked the Road, weren't there? Adventure. Danger, definitely danger."

"That is of no interest."

Lan knew Krek didn't mean that.

"The excitement provided us with grand memories. None of it can compare to sitting here for long hours and studying the perfection of your web treasure, though."

"That is true," Krek agreed. A while later, the spider asked, "How long would I be away from my lovely web if I went on this mad venture with you?"

"Not long, if we are successful and defeat Claybore. But if we fail...."

Krek pondered this. "There is no way I can consider such a crack-brained journey unless friend Inyx accompanies us. You will abandon me at the first opportunity, as you did before."

"No, Krek, I won't," protested Lan.

"And," the spider went on, ignoring Lan's outcry, "I want her to be there to give me some much-needed solace. She is quite good at that, for a human."

"I'd like her along, too," Lan said, mentally adding, *I need her with me*. "But she might refuse."

"Granted," said Krek, as if discarding such a silly notion outright. "What of that lumpy female who moons around and then tries to slit your puny throat?"

Sweat poured down Lan's chest, neck, and face as the spider reminded him of Kiska d'Adesina. The geas grew more powerful by the minute. He fought down the irrational urge to leave Krek and return immediately to be at Kiska's side. He cursed Claybore for this, even as he tried to calm himself and deny the magical bonds.

"I see you are still attached to her." Krek rocked his head from side to side. "What bizarre mating rituals you humans have. And yet you claim to find it odd that Klawn was supposed to eat me, or cocoon me for our hatchlings."

"Claybore's compulsion spell is too strong now for me

to break. This is another reason I need your help, Krek. I cannot prevent Kiska from harming me at the times I am most vulnerable."

"Yet you would fry me if I tried to harm her."

"Yes." Lan swallowed hard, but he had to let Krek know his problems.

"When do we leave?"

"What?"

"Is even your hearing faulty? I would have thought disuse would have quieted the ringing in your ears. While you will never have the acute hearing and vibratory sensing of a spider, I had thought . . ."

"You'll come with me?" Lan asked, startled at the sudden acceptance.

"I said as much. Now do we go to find friend Inyx, or do we malinger in the cave only to admire that pathetic wall hanging?" Krek indicated his finely spun web.

Lan and Krek *popped!* into the world in the midst of a battle. Lan reacted instinctively, drawing sword and bringing it downward in a long, powerful slash that ended a grey legionnaire's life. He had to put his foot on the man's chest to give enough leverage to pull his blade free. By the time he spun about, ready to continue the fight, he saw that Krek had been actively eliminating soldiers. The sight of the giant arachnid implacably snipping and clacking his way through their ranks demoralized them.

They broke rank and ran—to their death.

Inyx gave the order to her slingers. As soon as the soldiers exposed themselves to fire, a hail of exploding pellets fell among them. Only a handful survived to surrender.

Lan panted harshly from the exertion. In prior times he would have just been getting started. Now he felt slow, tired, out of place.

"Friend Lan Martak," complained Krek. "Why did you not use a spell to reduce them all to quivering blobs of green slime or some other appropriate measure?"

"Didn't think of it," Lan admitted. But he had noticed

Krek again referred to him as "friend." That lent more strength to his arm than anything else might have.

"They're all dead," Krek said, almost sadly. He was ready for a fray and it was at an end.

"What brings you here to ruin our carefully laid plans?" asked Ducasien.

"I come to speak with Inyx," Lan replied.

"She is busy with planning for the final thrust at the grey-clads' heart. All save one of their fortresses have fallen and the remaining one is poorly supplied. A siege might bring it down with little injury to our rank."

"I need to speak with her," Lan repeated. He used just enough of the Voice to convince Ducasien of the seriousness of the matter.

"I will tell her."

"Take us to her," Lan ordered. Ducasien obeyed, knowing he was being manipulated magically. Lan did not care for the man who had become Inyx's lover and cared even less if Ducasien knew he was being manhandled by minor spells. Once more Lan felt time pressing in all around him. The Resident of the Pit had to be released—soon.

"Lan!" Inyx cried. She forced herself to calm and said in a less enthused voice, "What are you doing here?"

"According to Ducasien, interfering with your plans."

"Krek!" Inyx ran to the spider and hugged two front legs. "It's so good to see you again."

"You are getting spots of my fur wet with your salty tears, friend Inyx. I wish you humans would not leak like that every time you show emotion."

"The fur's grown back well. No signs of the burns," Inyx said, stroking over the bristly front leg.

"It has been a considerable time since we parted," Krek said. "On the world where I became Webmaster of the mere spiders, it has been almost four years."

"So long! It's only a few months here," said Inyx.

"And about the same for me," said Lan.

Inyx tried to ignore him but couldn't. "How have you been, Lan?"

"Missing you," he said.

"Inyx. We must reinforce the troops to prevent any from escaping the fortress," said Ducasien.

"Do it," ordered Lan, the Voice again compelling Ducasien to obey.

The man trotted off to carry out the order.

"Don't use the Voice on him like that, Lan. I don't like it."

"I won't on you, Inyx. I never have."

Inyx brushed back tangled strands of her raven-wing black hair with both hands. Her blue eyes locked with Lan's brown ones. The rapport that had once been theirs returned.

"Oh, Lan," cried Inyx, flinging herself into his arms. "It's been so damned hard. And I see what it's been like for you. Our thoughts. I mean, they linked like before, only, but . . . oh, damn!"

"Perhaps friend Inyx would care for a juicy bug to replenish all the fluids she is losing," suggested Krek.

"Everything's all right, Krek. Now."

"No, Lan. You don't understand how it is now." Inyx forced herself away. "Ducasien and I, we're a team. When you left—drove us away!—I needed someone and he was there. I can't do to him what you did to me. I just can't. It wouldn't be fair."

Lan explained his need, how only Inyx could provide the support he needed to penetrate the spells guarding the Pillar of Night and counter it to release the Resident.

"The fight is almost complete here. We can't leave without making sure that the greys can never regain their power."

"Inyx, Claybore will become a god. Do you think minor battles mean anything to him? He fights for all the worlds along the Road, not just one. He can afford to let you expend your effort here while winning a thousand others."

"We're only human, Lan. We can only deal with one at a time." She looked at him, her blue eyes probing. "Ducasien and I are humans. Are you?"

Lan had no answer for her. He ever feared thinking about it. Too often he had been told he was immortal. His magical abilities far transcended any controlled by a mage, other than Claybore. Did this make him less than human—or more?

"Friend Lan Martak is sincere," said Krek. "There is even a shred of logic to his plan to enlist the aid of this former god."

"We need the Resident, Inyx," he said. "With his aid we can defeat Claybore once and for all."

"Terrill thought so, too."

Lan knew he'd have to tell her of Terrill's fate later.

"In this, I am right. We can defeat Claybore."

"Very well," she said cautiously. "You convince me, but only because of one thing."

"What's that?" Lan asked.

"You're saying 'we' instead of 'I' when you talk of stopping Claybore. That's the only way I'll aid you—as an equal."

"Three equals," said Lan, looking over at Krek and smiling.

"Four," said Ducasien, returning in time to overhear. "I do not like this, I think you lead us all to death, Martak, but I will not allow Inyx to go anywhere I do not also go."

"As four equals," Lan said. He and Ducasien shook hands. Inyx laid her hand atop theirs and over their heads came a long, hairy leg. They would fight as one in the final confrontation.

CHAPTER FOURTEEN

Claybore walked down the corridor, his bowed leg giving him a curiously rolling gait. The mage held onto his left arm as it tried to fall off once more, and his skull actually split enough to drop a tiny piece to the wooden flooring. Claybore bent and picked up the precious skull fragment and gently put it back into place. With some reluctance, it stayed.

In spite of all the troubles he experienced with his newly whole body, Claybore felt more power surging within him than he had since Terrill had dismembered him. The circuit had been completed, albeit imperfectly. The magics long lost now sang and pulsed through his veins. The sorcerer felt invincible, like a god.

"Patriccan!" he called out. "Attend me!"

Patriccan's own wounds had healed adequately for the man to show little outward sign of damage. He hastened to join his master.

"How may I be of service?" he asked, bowing low. Patriccan winced at the sight of the dark eye sockets churning with the pale ruby light. The death beams that lashed forth had reduced the ranks of his mages by a quarter. None stood against that ravening death—none except Lan Martak.

"My arm rejects me once again. Is there nothing to do? A demon to summon?"

"Master, even at the best of times it is difficult to entrap a demon. Since you exiled the one who worked on your leg, they have become even wilier in eluding my snare spells. Hasn't the adhesive paste bonded the arm?"

"See for yourself." Claybore thrust out his left shoulder. The arm had disconnected grotesquely and dangled by a few arteries and grey, stringy nerves.

"Please, master, come into my laboratory. I will again attempt the connection. The flesh has been separated so long that it has taken on a life of its own."

"One of the penalties of immortality. The parts attempt to live by themselves. Damn Terrill," Claybore exclaimed. Then the sorcerer chuckled and danced about, favoring his gimpy leg. "How should I visit Terrill and let him know that his plight will continue? How can I best instill hope and then dash it?"

"His madness prevents any such revenge, master," said Patriccan fumbling with the arm. He frowned. The best of his magics failed to hold Claybore's arm in place. Even Claybore had not been able to keep himself intact.

"Perhaps I shall lift the madness, give the promise of rescue—after letting him know what his life has been like for ten thousand years—and then cast him back into insanity."

"A fitting end for him, master."

"Don't patronize me, fool." Claybore jerked free of Patriccan's fumbling examination. He stormed into the journeyman mage's laboratory and perched on the edge of the green-tiled table, waiting impatiently.

Patriccan went first to a cabinet filled with vials and mixed a new potion. He chanted over it and activated it with magics barely under his control.

"This will keep the arm from slipping free of its own volition," said Patriccan. He held Claybore's arm in place, then swabbed on the frothy mixture he had conjured.

"My arm turns increasingly numb. No feeling and the fingers refuse to clench."

"Master, this is the best I can do. Will you do battle with Martak soon? If I have time to experiment, perhaps then I can find some other way of mending your body."

"The power is on me," said Claybore. "Simply having all my parts again augments my ability. Spells long forgotten now return to me, and power? I have *power!*"

Patriccan looked skeptically at the mage. The bone white of the skull had been broken by the weblike dark fracture patterns. The flesh had been destroyed and the tongue now rested in Martak's mouth. Patriccan did not understand how Claybore could be so sanguine about his chances when the reconstructed body that carried him into this conflict betrayed him at every turn.

"Come into the viewing room, Patriccan," ordered Claybore. "I will show you the progress I make."

Patriccan followed, feeling the aches in every joint; but compared to his master, he was in perfect condition.

"See?" said Claybore, pointing to the wall of moving scenes. "On that world the conquest is complete. A full score of sorcerers joins the effort. On this world, two of my strongest opponents are dead. Their magics availed them nothing." Claybore chuckled when he saw huge mechanical juggernauts, magically powered by captive demons, lumbering forth to crush opposition. This world had proven especially recalcitrant. Only the most intricate of magics had allowed Claybore to topple its regime.

"And there," the mage continued, rubbing hands together as he stood in front of one panoramic view of a world in ruins, "there my troops have captured a grimoire, that might allow me to complete the spell creating the Pillar of Night."

"You would kill the Resident?"

"Perhaps, perhaps not," said Claybore. "I am undecided. I rather enjoy gloating, and the Resident of the Pit is a captive audience this way. Still, I prefer having the power to permanently remove a god, if the mood strikes me. The legion commander on that world will deliver the grimoire to me within the week."

"What efforts are being made by Martak? I cannot assume he bides his time."

"There is evidence he penetrated all the way to the Pillar," said Claybore. "I have not been able to contact k'Adesina and find out. The Lady Brinke holds Kiska behind a wall of magic."

"You cannot break through?" asked Patriccan, astonished.

"Of course I can." Claybore's irritation made Patriccan cringe away. He waited for the ruby death beams. They never came. "I have been occupied with other things." Claybore flexed his right arm; his left sluggishly stirred but did no more.

Patriccan, for the first time, began to doubt. His master took too many chances, made too many mistakes. While Claybore was ostensibly whole again, Patriccan knew how tenuous were the bonds holding arms and legs to the torso. The dismembered sorcerer gained much in strength by being reassembled, but all of the parts were not his own. Did that cause the peculiar overconfidence? Patriccan hoped not. The final confrontation with Martak required every skill Claybore had accumulated over a very long lifetime of sorcerous doings.

"It will all come together on the plains in front of the Pillar of Night," said Claybore. "Martak will not stand a chance. And with his defeat, I will sap the power that makes him so powerful. I will suck up his essence and let it fill me. I will become the new god of the universe. None will dare oppose me!"

"None so dares now, master," said Patriccan.

"Martak does. Look. There and there and there." Claybore went from scried scene to scene, pointing. "All those worlds opposed me. They were crushed by might of arms. No longer will they even *think* of opposition. My very name will cause them to drop to one knee and pay me the homage I am due."

"Those machines," said Patriccan. "They come to this world? How? Surely, none will fit through a cenotaph."

"They come," said Claybore. "Using this, they will come." He tapped his chest cavity where the Kinetic Sphere pulsed slowly.

Patriccan said nothing. He knew the immense power of the Kinetic Sphere, but the journeyman mage had to question the value of Claybore's draining himself so before meeting Martak. The effort to move even one of those huge demon-powered fighting machines from another world had to be extreme.

He bowed and left the room. There were preparations to be made and perhaps he might even find the time to properly question a few prisoners brought him from another world. He had no desire for the information they hid; Patriccan desired only the painful questioning.

That would ease some of the strain he felt, he was positive.

"Why not just fly directly to the Pillar?" asked Ducasien as they disembarked from the demon-powered flyer. The warrior was still pale from the trip; it was his first experience with such a vehicle and the demon had berated him constantly for his airsickness.

"I tried that before," said Lan. "The demon refused to go any closer than the edge of the forest. But I have a path well scouted now. The dangers of the forest are . . . minimal."

All knew Lan lied. The sense of "deadness" within the woods reflected a closer appraisal of their chances. But Lan was able to use his spells freely enough now and that opened ways that were both more and less dangerous. The physical threat within the sterile forest would be small, but the attention attracted by the use of a potent spell might be unwanted. It was a risk that had to be borne.

"You leave me sitting here," complained the demon within the flyer. "Just like that? After so many hours of faithful service? What kind of ass are you?"

"Be quiet or I shall eat you," said Krek. The spider

unfolded long legs from the cramped storage space of the flyer. One taloned leg tapped hard against the hatch plate behind which the demon crouched.

"Go on, you overgrown nightmare. Try it! I'll give you such a case of heartburn you'll never recover!"

"We have no time for such things, Krek." Inyx tugged at the giant arachnid's leg and led him away.

"All things being equal, I would rather devour her." Krek's mandibles clacked just inches away from Kiska k'Adesina's neck. The mousy-appearing woman's expression altered in a flash and her long sword snaked from its sheath, point darting straight for the spider. Lan was helpless to stop her, but Brinke wasn't.

The blonde raised her arm and blocked the thrust so that it missed Krek's thorax by inches. Brinke mouthed a small spell that made Kiska drop to her knees, cursing volubly.

"You blonde bitch. You will die for this. My legs are numb. Lan, I can't walk!"

"Release the spell, Brinke." Lac closed his eyes and tried to retain his calmness. How could he possibly do battle with Claybore when his handful of supporters tried to slay one another—and the ones who weren't actively working toward killing merely hated the others.

"Very well." The lovely mage passed her hand above the fallen woman's head. Hair began to sizzle and spark. The smell of burned hair filled the air and gave some substance to the undead forest.

"Stop it!" Lan shouted, control gone.

Ducasien moved to stand beside Inyx, hand on sword. Brinke flinched but stopped her spell. Even Krek shifted away. Lan had used the Voice, something he had avoided among the group before this.

"We have little time. Bickering among ourselves will only lead us to defeat."

"She will stab you in the back at the first opportunity," said Brinke, pointing to Kiska. The brown-haired commandant of Claybore's troops smiled wickedly.

"I know," Lan said weakly.

"We still have time, Lan my darling," Kiska said, rising to her feet. She stroked along his cheek and kissed him. She clung to him and prevented him from getting away. He lacked the resolve to make her stop, even though he knew both Inyx and Brinke were seething.

"Put her into the chamber with the demon," suggested Krek. "Let them give one another heartburn."

"No way, you oversized ceiling crawler," protested the demon. "It's too damn small in here. First you want me to fly right on up to that awful black rotating pillar and risk my scaly limbs. Now you want to squeeze a truly dreadful lumpy human in here with me. You're a cruel one, fuzz-legs."

"Thank you," said Krek. "I had not expected such a fine compliment from one of your inferior mental status."

"Inferior!" raged the demon. It scrabbled against the metal plates until a loud ringing echoed through the forest. The spells binding it to the flyer were too great. After a few minutes of frenzied activity, the demon subsided into a sulky silence.

"We must hurry," said Lan, not using the Voice now. He already felt drained and the real struggle had yet to begin. Just trying to hold together this disparate band taxed him to the utmost.

The flow of emotion became too confusing for him to consider. Ducasien loved Inyx, who obviously cared for him—but little more. Brinke had true affection for Lan, but the sorcerer tried to hold back because the geas forced him to unwanted behavior toward Kiska. Kiska hated them all, but experienced some of the geas toward Lan so that she would only wait for the worst possible instants before trying to assassinate him.

Lan's head threatened to split like a frozen spring melon.

"Yes, let us leave this posturing device," said Krek. The spider *thwacked!* the side of the flyer before joining Lan.

"Krek, you, Inyx and Ducasien will have to fend off any physical attacks. Brinke and I will concentrate on the sorcerous ones—and they are going to be desperate ones."

"Will Claybore throw everything against us before we get to the Pillar of Night?" asked Inyx. "Or will he let the forest wear us down before attacking?"

"This is a mistake," cried Kiska. "Lan works to release Claybore's soul. It's trapped by the Pillar!"

Lan cut off the protests from Brinke even as they formed on the woman's lips. "I know," the man said. "She lies. I have felt the Resident of the Pit within."

"It's a trap," insisted Kiska. "Claybore is gulling you into believing you aid the Resident."

Lan started walking, trying not to listen to the bickering that flowed around him. By the time the first wave of mutilated forest-dwellers swung down on them, the petty arguments had ceased.

"Aloft!" cried Ducasien. "In the trees!"

His sword whispered free of its engraved leather sheath and skewered an armless woman as she slithered down a vine, using only legs and incredibly powerful teeth for support. Inyx quickly responded and drove off another seeking their blood—or was it another pair? The two men were joined at the side, sharing two heads, and the proper number of limbs for a single human.

"How revolting," said Inyx. "Killing them makes me feel dirty."

"They will kill us if we don't," pointed out Ducasien. He bound a wound on his arm himself as they hurried on. "Vicious fighters."

"Demented fighters," said Lan. "Claybore has driven them all quite mad."

"He experimented horribly upon them," said Brinke, shivering delicately. "And . . . Lan! Do you sense it?"

Lan kept walking but summoned up the light mote familiar he had cultivated into his major offensive and defensive weapon. The mote whirled forth, spun through the forest in a crazy orbit and returned seconds later. On the rippling surface of the point of light Lan read the spells forming around them.

He began counters immediately.

"The ground!" shouted Kiska. "Run!"

"Stand," said Lan. "It is illusion."

The yawning chasm split open the soft earth, sucking in trees and scores of the screeching remnants of Claybore's experiments. The pit looked endless—and it widened, moving toward the small group with a dizzying speed.

"Run. It'll swallow us all. Run," urged Kiska.

Lan lifted the light mote and brought it hurling downward at his feet. The bright pinpoint burned through the ground at the vee front of the pit. The hole vanished.

"Illusion," insisted Lan.

"Lan," Brinke said, clinging to his arm. "Something moves against us."

"The trees. They are Claybore's creatures. I hold them at bay."

"No, you're failing. They're coming for us. The trees will destroy us." Kiska bolted and tried to run. Lan felled her with a simple spell, then ran to her side.

"Are you all right?" he asked, concerned—and hating himself for it. This woman was a cold-blooded killer and had proven it on a dozen worlds.

"No," she sobbed. "Turn back. Now, Lan, for me."

His vision blurred and his mouth turned dry. Only Inyx's hand on his shoulder kept him from passing out.

"We must continue," the dark-haired woman said in a soft voice. Electricity flowed through her light touch on his shoulder, and they both trembled as the rapport that had once been theirs built anew. More than words, they shared emotions, inchoate thoughts, the most subtle of communications.

Kiska saw the sharing between them and moved to kill Lan. Inyx swung her fist and clipped the other woman on the point of the chin even as Lan acted to stop her.

Kiska lay unconscious on the ground. Lan apologized to Inyx.

"Lan, please," Inyx said. "I . . . we." She took a deep breath. "I understand the power of this compulsion now that we can again see into one another's souls."

"You see why I went astray?" he asked.

Inyx nodded.

"I thought I didn't need you. I was wrong. I need you in all ways."

"Will you two please explain this mating ritual to me?" piped up Krek. "I have tried in vain to understand it. You, friend Inyx, must knock down the scrawny one so that friend Lan Martak can..."

"Never mind, Krek."

"But I do wish to explain this to my hatchlings. They must deal with you ridiculous humans." The spider canted his head to one side. "I rather wish to understand it myself and I am failing."

"Let's march," said Ducasien. His gruff tones told how little he liked seeing Inyx with Lan. "We can leave her." He indicated Kiska with the tip of his sword.

"She comes along," said Lan before he could stop himself.

"Bring her," Inyx said. "It's all right, Ducasien. I begin to understand the magics involved."

Ducasien hoisted Kiska over his shoulder, muttering about clean steel and fair fights.

"The magics still surround us," said Brinke. "They overwhelm me. I can't fight them."

Krek stopped and faced the white-haired man in a small clearing. "Do let us by," said the spider, "or I shall be forced to eat you."

Terrill waved his hand. Krek collapsed against a tree, which immediately began dropping leaves and sinuous vines down around his stilled body.

"You can't stop us," said Lan. "Have you remembered or does Claybore only use you?"

"My friends are all so peeved that their rest is disturbed," said Terrill. The madness burned in his eyes, brighter than Lan had seen it before. "They want you to leave. Go now and don't bother us further. We are preparing for a party. Oh, yes, a fine party. None of you is invited."

"This is Terrill?" asked Inyx, eyes wide. "I had expected more."

"The spells are overwhelming me," said Brinke. "Help me, Lan. I'm being drowned in a sea of magic."

The blonde mage pulled her regal scarlet cloak tighter around her sleek body. Then all movement ceased. She stood as still as any marble sculpture. Ducasien and Inyx were similarly disabled. Lan saw Ducasien's eyes turn wild with despair.

"You are a great sorcerer, Terrill. The greatest who ever lived. You once aided the Resident of the Pit. Do so now. Help us free him from under the Pillar."

"Pinned there, the god's pinned there. Not killed, oh no, Claybore couldn't do that. But the years . . . so many years." For a moment Lan thought he had reached the deranged sorcerer.

"You must go," Terrill said. "Now!" He waved his hand and set a cascade of fire tumbling forth from his fingertips. Lan's light mote expanded to shield him and the others.

"Claybore animates you," Lan said. "Fight him. You can again be the mage you were. Decent, wanting only freedom. Fight Claybore."

"Rook!" screamed Terrill. "Destroy them all!"

The trees moved aside for the mud and stick figure striding through the sterile forest. Leaves fluttered in mock applause for their champion. Sap oozed like drool from the mouth of a fool.

And Lan Martak feared Terrill's champion.

Rook no longer stood a few inches high. He was Lan's height and more. The clay flesh had firmed and rippled with underlying muscle. The parody of a face sneered: rock eyes turned into black pools of hatred; cheek bones of twigs lifted into a squint; the simple gash mouth opened to reveal a whiteness Lan was only too familiar with.

It was the absolute whiteness found between worlds. Inyx had been lost in it and Claybore had tried to exile Lan once into that infinity. Now another creature of Claybore's threatened them with it.

"Destroy them all, Rook," shrieked Terrill.

Lan set his most powerful fire spell against Rook. Nothing happened. Conjuring an air elemental, the whirlwind whipping about the mud creature's stick feet, did not even slow its inexorable pace. Opening a pit in front of Rook did nothing. It walked on emptiness.

"Brinke," pleaded Lan. "I need your energy." He did not find it. The woman's entire being was tangled in Terrill's immobility spell.

But help came. A feeble grasping at first firmed into something more substantial. Lan experienced it as a hand on his back, urging him forward, comforting him, giving him the courage to fight.

"Inyx," he said softly. "Thank you."

Rook's bulging, sapling arms circled Lan's body. Mud muscles tightened. The mouth opened to whiteness and turned to rip out his throat.

Lan Martak concentrated all his power into the light mote. His body slumped in Rook's arms, more a corpse than lifelike. But the magical energies flowed like a mighty river. With Inyx's encouragement and succor, Lan focused them into a stream of incalculable power. And this he refined into the single mote of light. It shot forward and into Rook's obscenely gaping mouth.

Flames seared Lan's eyebrows and hair. He stumbled back and fell heavily. Dried sticks and mud rained down on him and with the physical came more. Broken spells, tangled magics, bits and pieces of a long lifetime of being a sorcerer all poured into him, like water into a bucket. Lan not only destroyed Rook, he shattered Terrill's mind once and for all time.

The burned out husk of a once-great mage stood in the clearing, all light gone from the eyes.

"He still lives," said Brinke, released from Terrill's spell. "But there is no life force."

"You're wrong," Lan said. "The life force is all that's left. Everything else has been drained. Terrill is, indeed, immortal and cannot be killed by ones such as we, but all that remains is a shell. He has no personality left, not even a deranged one. No volition, no sense of being alive."

"How horrible," muttered Ducasien.

"This might be a better existence than the one Claybore doomed him to," said Inyx. "But I don't think so. Lan, can you do anything for him?"

Lan didn't answer. All the knowledge that had been sealed and unreachable in Terrill's mind now unfolded for him. His powers doubled, trebled—more!

"I can do nothing," Lan said. "That is still beyond my grasp." He stretched out a hand to Inyx, who took it. Her eyes welled with tears as she saw within him the truth of all he said.

"He is surely doomed to be like this forever," Inyx said. "The poor, poor man."

"Friend Lan Martak," came Krek's shaky voice. "Behind you is the terrible woman. She again tries to do you harm. If you let her, can you then mate? This is so odd, backwards from the way we spiders do it. We mate first, then the female devours the male."

Lan had forgotten about Kiska k'Adesina in the aftermath of the brief, mind-twisting battle with Terrill's golem. He moved the barest fraction of an inch, not even taking his hand from Inyx's, and let Kiska's dagger pass harmlessly by his back.

Kiska spun like a jungle beast, dagger held point up in a knife-fighting position.

The snarl of feral rage on her face showed that she thought the time ripe for killing Lan.

Lan motioned for the others to hold.

"Kiska," he said in a low voice, "you have tried to kill me for the last time."

"Yes," she hissed. "This time I succeed! And if they stop me, you'll present the opportunity again for me to drive my knife into you, you weak, sniveling fool."

She lunged and again Lan sidestepped.

"You can't prevent me from killing you, can you, you lovesick bastard?"

"The geas Claybore laid upon me is a subtle and complicated one," said Lan. "I have to admit to a certain admiration for the delicacy of the spell and the way Claybore wrapped it around my own vanity, ego, and need to best him. Yes, that's what he did," said Lan to Inyx. "As much as anything else, the geas fed my ego, making me think I was invincible." He gave a tired little laugh.

"The irony of it is that I *am* invincible. Now."

"Not to me, Martak. You love me. You love the source of your own death!"

Kiska viciously drove the dagger tip directly for Lan's groin. The blade vaporized, taking with it her hand, wrist and most of her forearm.

"Yes, Kiska, I suppose I do still love you. The geas is strong, but I am now stronger. Terrill's legacy to me."

Kiska stared stupidly at her ruined hand. Her brown eyes lifted to Lan's and a frightened look came into them. Lan made a small motion and Kiska k'Adesina fell to the ground, dead.

"You killed her." Ducasien stared at the woman's still body.

Brinke gasped and turned shades whiter. She put one hand over her mouth and backed from Lan.

Lan felt only sorrow for Kiska. She had been little more than a pawn in this world-spanning power game.

But Lan felt even sorrier for Brinke. She possessed enough knowledge to understand what he had become. And for Inyx, who *saw* inside him. She *saw* what he was still changing into.

"The real conflict lies ahead of us," Lan said. "We can reach the Pillar of Night in a few minutes, if we hurry."

CHAPTER FIFTEEN

Lan Martak heard them whispering about him as he strode forward. The awful forest silence became more and more oppressive to him and the small, half-heard words irritated him.

"Either speak your mind or stay silent," he snapped.

"Lan?" Inyx fell into step beside him. "You're acting as you did before. We all want to help."

He looked into her blue eyes and saw nothing but admiration and love there. He fought to hold himself in check.

"You know how I feel? About Kiska?"

Inyx nodded.

Lan looked ahead, not wanting to meet her eyes. "I hate myself for killing her, but if any of you had done it, I couldn't have stopped myself from exacting revenge. Claybore is a subtle monster. The geas still binds me."

"She is dead."

"I still love her."

Inyx put her arm around his shoulder. When he tried to shrug it off, muscles as strong as any steel band tightened. Lan stopped fighting it and they walked on like this, not speaking. The time for words was long past between them. The communication flowed in both directions, but the power resided mostly within Lan's mind. Inyx carried some small measure of his energy, his ability, but it was a weak reflection. She understood what he did—and why—but could not work those spells herself. Her part was to give him stability. He trod areas that had driven others insane. Inyx lent support and a firm basis from which to act, but the action itself had to well up from inside Lan Martak.

"We need the Resident," he said.

"I know. Are you really so concerned about releasing him?"

"He was a god once, until Claybore stole his powers. I do not want the Resident wreaking vengeance on all humanity because of something Claybore alone has done."

"He knows who is responsible."

"But he's a god and who can say what a god thinks?"

Inyx tightened her arm around Lan's waist.

"No!" Lan snapped. "I am *not* a god. You know that. Look at me and tell me I'm not a god, also."

"I can't, Lan. What is within you is so much more than human it frightens me. Even knowing you as I do, I'm scared."

"Friend Lan Martak," called out Krek. "These odious vines are dribbling sap all over my legs. Can we not get free of this silly forest?"

"Soon, Krek. The Pillar of Night is close."

"I know that," the spider said testily. "I sense it just as I do the cenotaphs. The moving trees crowd in on me and there are not any good grubs or bugs to be found. I think I shall certainly starve to death unless we find some soon."

"You wolfed down huge numbers of those grubs back on the other world, Krek. How can you be hungry again?"

Krek sniffed. "Kadekk might have been right. This whole venture is looking more foolhardy by the moment. She had a way about her, Kadekk did, even if she was only a mere spider."

Inyx looked questioningly at Lan. "The spider he left in

charge," Lan explained to her. "Krek was Webmaster and had to delegate his authority to one of them. This Kadekk was the most capable."

"She spun a fine web," said Krek, "but certainly not one as fine as I. Friend Inyx, you should have seen my web treasure. A masterpiece. None like it for texture or intricacy of pattern."

Lan stopped. Inyx's arm tensed, then dropped away. The dark-haired woman stepped back beside Ducasien. Even she felt the radiance, the malevolence ahead.

"The Pillar of Night," Brinke said. The regal blonde woman stopped beside Lan. Inyx wanted to go join Lan, but even the rapport she had with the mage wasn't enough to be of any help. Only another adept might give him the keys he needed to unlock this terrible spell cast by Claybore so long ago.

"What are they doing?" asked Ducasien. "What are we supposed to do?"

"We wait. You and me and Krek. Our job is done now. Theirs has just started."

Ducasien fingered his sword and stood on tiptoe to peer through the trees to see what Lan and Brinke already "saw."

"That's it? Even when we were coming to this infernal forest in the belly of that infernal machine, I saw nothing."

"The blackness," said Krek. "That is the Pillar of Night."

Ducasien stayed unimpressed until Lan gestured and the trees reluctantly began moving away at the command. Then the warrior's attention riveted to the vast black expanse rising up.

Lan hastened the trees to one side and walked forward, his mind reaching out to lightly touch the surface of the Pillar. Brinke beside him, they stopped only a few feet from the light-devouring column. Lan looked up and experienced a few seconds of vertigo. The Pillar was so tall it appeared to be leaning out, toppling over. But the moving spikes atop it helped Lan get the proper perspective. He blinked a few times and all became clear.

All.

"Resident of the Pit," he said, "we have come to release you."

"I see your intent, Lan Martak. Free me, yes, but let me die. I have grown too weary to continue this existence."

"We need your aid to conquer Claybore and his armies," Brinke said. "You cannot refuse us."

"Give me my wish and I shall do whatever I can to help."

Lan did not speak. His mind worked over complex relations, spells, laws both mundane and arcane. The unlocking would be easier than he had thought. He had accumulated knowledge from so many sorcerers. Abasi-Abi on Mount Tartanius. Some of the gnome sorcerer Lirory Tefize's grimoires. All the spells locked within Terrill's mind. Even spells accompanying Claybore's tongue. Lan swallowed and tasted the bitter metal in his mouth. It sickened him even as it fed him power, knowledge, confidence. Coupled with the lore gained from those sources, Lan's own experimentations had built up an arsenal of magic unparalleled since the time of the Resident.

It was still not enough to defeat Claybore unaided. He needed the Resident of the Pit.

"Lan," said Brinke, her voice husky with fear. "Claybore's legions. They mass on the plains." She pointed. Lan looked over his shoulder and tried not to panic.

Never had he seen such an array of fighting men and machines. The forest had been silently sliding open to leave an unimpeded path for the mage's army. Ten miles distant stood rank upon rank of armored might.

"The huge rolling fortresses are demon-powered fighting machines," he said. "I feel the resentment of the demons spell-trapped within."

"They spit fire," cried Ducasien. "How can we fight those?"

Lan and Brinke turned to face the army advancing upon them. Long tongues of flame erupted from the blunted snouts of the machines. The demons spewed forth their wrath at being penned within the bellies of the machines and the mages guiding the machines opened vents to release the fire. Trees five miles distant from the leading machine exploded in a fireball.

"They kill at such a distance," Inxy said. "Lan?"

"We can fight them. These are sent only to unnerve us."

"The fire," came Krek's quaking voice. "My furry legs will go up just like tinder. Oh, friend Lan Martak, if Claybore means to frighten me, he has succeeded!"

Lan glanced at Krek and flashed him a reassuring smile. The giant arachnid refused to be consoled. Lan took a deep breath and settled his mind. The spells rose at his command, like bubbles in a pond. As they burst, he cast them forth to do their worst.

The machine in the lead shook as if caught by a huge, invisible fist. Armor plates and metallic components exploded in all directions as Lan released the demon within.

"The others come faster. I feel the fire on my legs already. Oh, why did I leave my safe web? Kadekk was not such a bad sort but I would have done a much better job as Webmaster. She will only taint my webbing, I am sure of it. Oh, woe!"

Inyx soothed Krek but when she reached out to Ducasien, he pulled away. The man's face had turned pale but he stood squarely facing the oncoming hordes of men and magics.

Another of the mechanical juggernauts blew apart. And another and another. By the time the leading components of Claybore's army reached the edge of the magic-haunted forest, only two of the machines still operated. Lan closed his eyes and sent the light mote familiar deep into one of the demon-powered devices. He began tormenting the already angered demon with the mote, sending it needles of pain, sheets of driving rain, blinding dust. Trapped in the narrow cavity of the fighting machine, the demon lashed out and caused the mage controlling it to veer. It rolled over hundreds of foot soldiers using its bulk for protection. Lan ignored the cries audible even at this distance and continued turning the machine back into Claybore's grey-clad legions.

"They do not break and run. They still advance," said Brinke.

"Claybore has not only trained them well, they fear him more than anything we can do to them." Lan smiled grimly, feeling no humor in what he was about to do.

Lan blasted the sorcerers in control of the remaining death machines and let the demons run free. They turned on those around them, snorting fire and crushing humans beneath the machines' bulk. Above dived flyers powered by fire elementals, intent on destroying the renegade machines. Huge gouts of flame lanced from the tail to propel the metal cylinders. The mages controlling these started into a shallow dive, then opened vents to the front. The flames lashed downward.

Lan staggered back as wave after wave of heat struck around him. His clothes began smouldering and his hair singed. He heard Krek moaning in pain and Inyx cursing. Of Brinke he saw and heard nothing. He reached out for her, both physically and magically, but the blonde woman was not there. Then he understood why.

She had been protecting him from hammer-rapid blows sent by thousands of mages assembled by Claybore for this express purpose. Brinke had tired too quickly and now some of those magical stabs and prods came through her protection.

Lan gasped with strain when he carried more of the burden himself. He dared not relax for an instant; too many attacks came at him from too many directions. The aerial assaults continued and required him to protect all on the ground from the fire elementals' wrath. The juggernauts rumbling around in death-dealing circles on the ground still allowed many troops past, grey-clad soldiers who would soon close on him. Worst of all was the hail of pinpricks from the assembled sorcerers. No one individual mage contributed more than a tiny sting of magic, but their aggregate wore on him increasingly.

"Brinke," he pleaded. "Give me some aid. Please!"

Through a red fog he saw the blonde lying on the ground in a heap. She was unconscious.

"Resident!" he called. "They are too many for me. Help me now."

"The Pillar of Night still holds me immobile, Lan Martak. I can do nothing but suggest, to tell you that nothing is impossible for one such as yourself."

Lan stopped trying to counter on all fronts. The grey-clad soldiers presented the least immediate danger. He concentrated on the flyers. Conjuring a water elemental in midair and inside a moving flyer proved a trick almost beyond his levels of skill. Almost.

The hindmost of the flyers simply vanished in an incandescent cloud of molten metal as water and fire elementals locked together within the bowels of the machine. Slowly at first, then with greater confidence and control, he sent forth the water elementals to extinguish the power sources on the flyers.

It almost destroyed him and the others.

The hundreds—thousands?—of mages battering away at him intensified their attack. And still he did not sense Claybore's presence. The mage used all these tactics to wear Lan Martak down. Lan let out a tiny sob of frustration when he saw how well it worked.

The flyers were gone and the land-gripping juggernauts had passed the time of usefulness, but he weakened with every passing instant. The sheer force of the opposition made his knees tremble and his vision blur. He reached out and touched the Pillar of Night.

"No, not yet. You cannot," warned the Resident. Lan discovered the trap in trying to tap the Resident for help in this way. The spell forming the huge black cylinder sucked away at his vital forces and left him even more enervated. He tried to pull back and could not. As if stuck in tar, his hand refused to budge.

"Do you know fear, Martak?" came Claybore's booming voice. "When you touched the Pillar, you summoned me. I knew then that you were defeated."

"No, no!" sobbed Lan, struggling to pull free. Everything worked against him. The pressure from the phalanxes of sorcerers increased. The grey-clad legions trooped ever closer. And Claybore began his assault.

The other attacks on Lan's mind and body paled in comparison. Claybore's skill, his cunning, his eons of experience all went into defeating Lan.

"You are only a country bumpkin who stumbled onto a few spells. A chant to make a campfire, a minor healing potion, those are your domain, Martak. This is mine."

If any one of the other mage's attacks had been a pinprick, Claybore's was a battering ram. Somehow, Lan reached inside and held. But strength fled rapidly.

"You lost your ally," gloated Claybore. "The Lady Brinke is no mage. She furnished you with false hope and nothing more."

Lan sank further into defeat. Depression mounted. His cleverest spells availed him nothing. Claybore hid behind the combined might of all his mages and only waited for his grey-clads to arrive—and they would. Soon.

"The Resident found out how strong I was ten thousand years ago. He and Terrill, like you, Martak, underestimated my ability."

Lan struggled up and fought like a cornered rat. He felt the curtains of magic part and individual mages became apparent to him. One or two he recognized personally from past encounters, but most he did not. At the forefront of this assemblage, though, Lan picked out Patriccan.

"Yes, he remembers you," said Claybore. "He hates you for all you've done. Patriccan even begs me to let him be the one who destroys you, but I have yet to decide on your fate. Would you like to roam my little forest for all of time, as Terrill does?"

"Resist," came the Resident of the Pit's single suggestion. Lan already did that and slipped by slow inches into oblivion.

"I am sure we can find other appropriate measures to take, if we think long enough on them. You have a curious resiliency when it comes to winning free of the space between worlds. I do not think it wise to maroon you there again. Some other fitting punishment for all the trouble you have caused me must be found."

Lan sagged to his knees, hand still frozen to the Pillar of Night.

Strong hands picked him up, locked under his arms and held him. A bristly limb the thickness of his thigh smashed down upon his hand, knocking it free of the Pillar. Lan coughed and wiped away dirt and sweat. Dimly he saw Inyx supporting him with Krek nearby.

"We're not abandoning you," said Inyx.

"Not after that hideous Claybore singed my lovely legs," added Krek.

Lan Martak had been wrong. He had thought Brinke, being a mage, would give him more support. The mental link with Inyx did more than the blonde sorceress ever had to shore up his defenses, to lend him strength. And curiously, he found himself also linked with Krek.

From Inyx he received strength and drive. From Krek came a spider's viciousness, which would have driven any human insane.

His spells, Inyx's drive, Krek's ferocity. He bound them all together and hid them inside his light mote familiar, waiting for the proper instant. As Claybore built his assault, the moment came.

Patriccan paused for the briefest of times; Lan struck there.

The journeyman mage let forth a bloodcurdling shriek as Lan formed a fire elemental in the man's stomach. The instant Lan released the elemental, Patriccan died. The other mages assembled in the room also perished, alleviating some of the pressure Lan felt. He quickly sought and destroyed those sorcerers not in Claybore's headquarters.

"The troops still approach," Lan heard Ducasien calling. The young mage had no time for mere soldiers. Claybore presented the gravest danger.

"What?" came the startled cry as Claybore realized Lan not only fought back again but had eliminated all the other mages. "You . . . you can't do that. No one can!"

Lan lashed out at Claybore, striving to dismember him as Terrill had done so many years earlier. One arm fell off, but the mage's power remained unscathed. Recovering, Claybore visited upon Lan nightmares come to life. Lan faced his own weaknesses, his fears, his regrets. Inyx's support helped but it was Krek's single-minded ferocity that carried Lan past the obscene thoughts from his own mind.

"You cannot stop me," shouted Claybore. "You are not powerful enough alone, and you can never free the Resident of the Pit. I will see to that!"

"Resist him," came the soft voice of the Resident. "You must!"

"The Resident has used you, Martak. You were only a pawn from the beginning. He thought you could give freedom. Nothing you've done has been because *you* wanted it. The Resident drove you."

Lan looked at Inyx, her dark hair fluttering in the hot wind blowing from the plains. Her brilliant blue eyes shone. Behind her towered Krek. Chocolate-colored eyes betrayed none of the unswerving ferocity lodged in that arachnid nature.

"You are wrong, Claybore. The Resident of the Pit might have thought I was a pawn, but I have become more." And with Inyx and Krek, he *was* more.

Much more.

Claybore's peculiarly assembled body appeared in front of the advancing soldiers. On misshapen legs the sorcerer came forth, body limned with a ruby aura. The white skull had cracked and one-quarter of the top was missing. Claybore carried the one arm with the other and the necrotic section around the Kinetic Sphere visibly decayed.

Lan trembled at the realization that this was his enemy.

"Both you and the Resident were wrong, Claybore. I don't need his help to defeat you. All the aid I need is with me, outside the spells forming the Pillar of Night."

Lan waved his arm out in a fanning motion. The thousands of grey-clad soldiers perished, not even knowing death visited them.

Inyx and Krek crowded closer. Lan countered another of Claybore's spells and returned it a thousandfold. Inyx's arm around him almost cut off his wind and Krek's clacking mandibles threatened to sever head from torso, but Lan needed their support, their strength, their love.

Claybore gave out a wordless scream as Lan's light mote familiar split into tiny shards and sliced through shoulders, hips, chest, neck. Claybore's parts crashed to the forest floor and twitched, trying to reassemble. Lan muttered spells of immense power, power that caused the ground to quake and the sky to froth over with lightning-wracked clouds.

"You cut him apart, just as Terrill did." The awe in Inyx's voice brought Lan around.

"I can do more than Terrill," said Lan. "I can destroy him totally. Not even a fragment of flesh will remain if I utter one spell." He touched the tip of the iron tongue within his mouth. This, too, would be rent apart, but it was a small price to pay for Claybore's destruction.

"Do it," urged Inyx. "It is all we've fought for."

"No," Lan said. "I destroyed his legs but I will not destroy the rest of him."

"But why not?"

Lan smiled savagely. "Thank Krek for that. I have learned too well from him."

"Doubtful," muttered the spider, "but who can say what form your current delusion takes?"

"Each of Claybore's parts retains awareness. Rudimentary, but it is there. He *knows* all that has happened to him and he feels the pain constantly."

"For all eternity?" asked Inyx. "That's awful."

"That's the punishment I decree for him. His parts are immortal and shall live minimal existence. Not a moment will go by when Claybore doesn't realize the full impact of his defeat."

"What's to keep him from rejoining himself, like he did this time?" asked Ducasien.

"Terrill wasn't efficient in the way he scattered the pieces. He allowed Claybore to grow in power as each new piece was attached. Seeing Claybore's problems gave me the idea. Never again can one piece be attached to another. He will always be as you see him now."

Lan Martak began the complex array of spells. For over an hour he conjured and chanted. One by one, the pieces of Claybore's body vanished until only the battered, fractured skull remained.

"Claybore, you understand what I have done?"

"It will take millennia, Martak, but I will have my revenge!"

"It will be untold millennia and you will still be unable to do anything," promised Lan.

Tiny red sparks sputtered deep in the eye sockets. Nothing else happened. Claybore's power had been stolen away permanently.

Lan opened up the whiteness between worlds and cast Claybore's skull into it.

"You defeated him without my aid," said the Resident of the Pit. "I have created more than I guessed."

"You created nothing," snapped Lan. "I ought to leave you under the Pillar of Night. Not once did you tell me what you planned. You used me."

"And I would have discarded you had the weapon proved unsatisfactory against Claybore," the Resident finished. "I harbor no shame on that score. You know full well that horror of an eternity without power. Otherwise you would not have doomed Claybore in the fashion you did.

"Free me. Free me and give me death. That was your promise."

"Lan, are you going to?" asked Inyx. "If the Resident has been so treacherous up till now, how can you trust him after you free him?"

Lan laughed. The Resident said, "Even though you are in rapport with him, you do not understand, do you? Lan Martak transcended all I had anticipated. He is a god, immortal and invulnerable. There is nothing I can do, even after being freed, to endanger him."

"Immortal?" asked Krek. "That means...."

"I will outlive you and Inyx," said Lan, his voice low. "I understand that. But I will also have the power of life and death."

"You can grant a former god death. You will free me and then do what Claybore originally intended. You will destroy me. Only you can slay a god."

The expression on Inyx's face defied description. She shook her head and backed away from Lan.

"I don't believe this. You . . . you can't be immortal. Not really. And a god? I *know* you, Lan. You're not a god. You're not perfect."

"Not even a god is perfect," said Lan. "I am proof of that. My weaknesses remain under the veneer of power."

"But it is awesome power," said the Resident of the Pit. "Free me and give me surcease from my centuries of impotence."

"I promise you that, Resident."

Lan found the spells hidden in the dim recesses of his mind. Whether left by Terrill or Claybore or some other mage, he had no idea. They might even have been his own creation. Lan set the Pillar of Night spinning, faster and faster. The spikes atop it began to elongate.

He heard someone gasp when lightning bolts arced from each spike and split apart the heavens. Clouds formed above and pelted down rain in a torrential fury. Lan built the power required to a higher level, then to another and another. The ground shook beneath his feet and began to disintegrate.

"You will reign forever, Lan Martak," cried the Resident of the Pit. "Your powers are infinitely greater than mine ever were. Free me. Free me!"

Wind of hurricane force whipped about them. In the distance came impenetrable black clouds trailing tornados. These magical storms ringed the Pillar of Night. The spells holding the Resident of the Pit began to yield to the onslaught of Lan's power. Elementals of all forms whistled and whispered, sizzled and sprayed against the light-sucking blackness of the column.

"It comes," moaned the Resident. "The pressure on me lightens."

"Foul weather," grumbled Krek. "Rain is matting my fur, and the lightning. I never liked it. Set my web afire once back in the Egrii Mountains." The giant spider gusted a deep sigh. "How I miss my lovely Klawn."

"Lan," Inyx shouted over the gale-force winds whipping about them. "I can't reach you anymore. What's happening?"

"The core of the planet is rising beneath us," said Lan. "You, Krek, and Ducasien must walk the Road. Do it now. Hurry."

"We won't leave you."

"Nothing will harm me. I promise that. Now go."

"But we don't know where a cenotaph is."

"There," Lan Martak said, pointing. "There's one I just created. Use it! Now!"

Winds pulled Inyx away from him. She tried to fight the gusts and failed. Driven into the cenotaph, she, Krek and Ducasien, holding a lifeless Brinke, stared at Lan. Alone he stood next to the ebony Pillar of Night.

But the color changed. No longer did the column retain all energy. It glowed internally and rose upward, ripping apart the sky with the rotating spikes.

The last thing Inyx saw before the cenotaph opened and carried them to another world was the orange fire inside the Pillar, a signal that Lan had cracked the planet's crust and released the immense energies of a molten core.

The Pillar of Night ceased to exist and, along with it, the entire planet. Storms of magic raged until only dust spun through the cosmos. And then even this vanished.

EPILOGUE

Lan Martak walked along the paved street, hardly recognizing the buildings. The Dancing Serpent had been razed, some ten years earlier, one old-timer sitting rocked back in a chair had told him. Hardly anyone else remembered the place and even the old man didn't remember Zarella. She had been just a bit before his time, or so he said. From the twinkle in his eye, though, Lan thought the old man remembered the stunning woman. Perhaps he had even visited her a time or two and was now reluctant to admit to such youthful indiscretions.

Lan looked at the new building gleaming in the sunlight. Some architect had gone wild with glass and gilt edging. The wood beams over the porch had been intricately carved and a sign dangled down proudly proclaiming two chirurgeons and a solicitor specializing in demonic law had offices inside.

"Outta my way, you blithering fool!" came the loud cry. Lan turned and looked down the street. Two drivers hunched over the steering sticks on their demon-powered cars. Huge puffs of white steam rose from one; the other's smokestack spewed forth heavy, oily black. The two raced by, nearly running over a pedestrian who wasn't as fleet of foot as he ought to have been.

Lan had to laugh. He remembered how the old sheriff had hated those Maxwell-demon-powered contraptions. Then the man sobered. The sheriff had died less than a month after Lan had walked the Cenotaph Road for the first time. The grey-clads had murdered him, or so Lan had been told. Kyn-Alyk-Surepta had vanished soon after, leaving still another, even worse, garrison commander. In only a year the soldiers had supplanted the weak deputy who had taken the old man's place.

Lan's sister's rapist and murderer had come to justice on another world. His fist tightened around the dagger hanging at his belt as he remembered the brief pleasure he had taken killing Surepta—and then the hollowness following the bloody act. There had been no sense of revenge, just as the Resident of the Pit had predicted. Lan's sister was still dead, the sheriff had not been properly avenged, and Surepta's death had set off the long chain of events leading to Kiska k'Adesina trying to murder him.

"The time flows get confusing," Lan said softly, thinking about Kiska and Surepta. They had been married by the time Lan killed the man, yet Surepta had left this world after Lan.

"Either pay rent or move," came a cold voice. Lan looked over his shoulder and saw a uniformed officer behind him. "We don't hold with drifters coming through town." The officer cocked his head to one side and asked, "You be leaving soon?"

"This is—was—my home," Lan said. "A long time ago. I'm just looking around. A lot has changed."

"One thing's still the same," said the law officer. "We don't want trouble."

Lan sensed the magics at the officer's control. He smiled. The man probably conjured small sparks from his fingers. There'd be a paralysis spell in case anyone got too rowdy. Even the reduction spell for execution. To be reduced to a smoldering puddle of lard. Lan shook his head.

He had ruined worlds with the wave of his hand. And once he had feared the old sheriff's reduction spell.

"You got anybody to vouch for you?"

"What? Oh, no, no one. Not now. I just wanted to see the homesite once more, before I left."

The law officer nodded curtly. The expression on his face told Lan that he expected this unwanted loiterer out of town as soon as possible. Otherwise, Lan might spend the night in jail. The idea amused Lan.

He strolled the streets, then turned toward the outskirts of town. They were farther away than he remembered. There were more people than he remembered, too. And all were strangers.

He came to a simple house sadly in need of repairs. Lan knelt down by the foundations and saw the sword cuts in the wood beams where he had tried to get out of the locked cellar in time to save his sister. Surepta had killed her while Lan struggled.

The house was unoccupied, long since deserted.

He didn't bother entering. Lan turned into the woods and noted the lumbering activity. He wandered old game trails and saw no spoor. The animals had fled the encroaching civilization and without a doubt moved higher into the el-Liot Mountains. A grey-green haze from numerous factories cloaked the horizon and prevented Lan from seeing those majestic peaks.

The path widened unexpectedly and he found himself poised on the edge of a rock quarry. Dozens of men worked heavy equipment below. Demons screeched out their curses at being forced to use talons to cut through the rock, but the mine superintendent was a competent mage; he kept the demons at work quarrying while the men lugged the stone to conveyors and hoisted it from the pit.

"What you want, stranger?"

"Just looking," said Lan. "I'll be moving on soon enough. I used to live around here, but the quarry is new."

"New," snorted the man. "Been here well nigh fifteen years."

"They use the demons well," Lan said.

"Damn nuisance, if you ask me, but then nobody does. I'm just a watchman."

"You make sure no one steals a block of stone?"

The man laughed. "By all the Lower Places, I wish that were it. Damn kids come in and get into trouble here. I make sure no one's hurt. A demon worked his way free of his binding spell a year back. Damn-fool kid cornered the poor frightened bugger and made it do his schoolwork before releasing it. The demon came back in tears, begging to go onto the cutters again." The watchman shook his head.

"This is all so strange to me," Lan admitted. "I'm not used to it."

"Seeing more and more of the demons and sprites," the man said, mistaking what Lan meant. "Better get used to them. They're the future, or so the mages say."

"They may be right." Lan stared at the bustle in the pit mine, then asked, "Could you direct me to the cemetery? It used to be about a mile that way, but everything else has changed so."

"Still there." The watchman peered at Lan curiously. "Anything wrong?"

"Nothing. Just that you reminded me of someone. But it couldn't be."

"I did come from here."

"You look a lot like a fella I knew close to twenty years ago. He got involved in a multiple murder when I was only about seven."

"I might be the one."

"Couldn't be. You're not more than three years older than he was then. Don't know what happened to him. Nice guy but he went sour and killed his lover and his sister."

"Lan Martak," Lan said.

"What? Yes! That's the name. Dar-elLan-Martak. Remember how my ma carried on for weeks about it. Scared the wits outta me. How'd you know the name?"

"I'm looking for his grave," Lan said. The vagaries of time flow between the worlds took its toll on him now. He was only a few years older while almost twenty had passed on his home. And still he was remembered as a murderer.

"Down that trail and on about a mile, as you said," the watchman told him.

"Thanks."

Lan started off, the smell of real forest around him re-vitalizing him. His tired body came alive once more and energy surged through his veins. He felt powerful enough to smash worlds again when he arrived at the perimeter of the cemetery.

The wall had been repaired and extended. He walked through the gate and immediately saw the sheriff's grave.

"Twenty years," Lan said, shaking his head. "You were a good man. I'm sorry you had to live to see the Claybore's grey-clads taking over." Lan winced at the sound of a flyer above him. Even that particular perversion had been discovered by his home world's mages.

Lan went and sat on a new grave, a cenotaph. His feet dangled into the crypt and he watched the bugs in the stone box vainly trying to scale the marble walls and escape.

"What are you watching, Lan?" came a soft voice. Inyx put her hand on his shoulder. He covered it with his own hand.

"The insects. It's amazing how I ignored even the simplest of things for so long. A life-and-death struggle goes on under our noses and we don't see it."

"There are others to take their place if they die," Inyx said. "That's the way it is."

"There is always another to take your place," said Lan. "Do you regret it?"

He laughed, rich and full and long. The humor inside came welling up and boiled over, real and heartfelt.

"Regret it? Never. The Resident of the Pit certainly does, though."

"Have you looked into the well? The one where you first contacted the Resident?"

"No. I have no desire to seek him out. He is a god again. I'm only a mortal."

"A mortal I love."

Lan and Inyx sat side by side watching the bugs tumbling and crawling, climbing and finally escaping the cenotaph. He knew the exultation they felt on attaining the rim of the cairn. It was precisely the way he felt when he realized he *was* a god and as such could do anything he desired.

Anything at all.

He had freed the Resident of the Pit by shattering the spells forming the Pillar of Night. The magma from the planet had burst upward and blown the black shaft far into space. The energies released were too great for any world to contain; the planet had been turned to rubble in one cataclysmic eruption.

He and the Resident had floated freely in space, no longer bound by body or planet. They belonged to the universe.

That was when Lan had refused to kill the Resident. Instead, he had meted out a punishment far worse than even that given to Claybore.

First had been a geas patterned after the one Claybore had so cunningly used on him. Lan applied it to the Resident, then he had relinquished all his power by transferring it to the Resident. Again the being became a god. Again the Resident of the Pit had to endure the worship of petty humans. Again the Resident became more than a pitiful, trapped creature.

And he could not kill himself or force the power back on Lan because of the geas.

Lan was happy to again have to walk the Cenotaph Road using the empty graves as his highway.

"One lifetime is enough," Lan said, "if it's done right." He kissed Inyx, relishing the feel of a real tongue moving against hers. Claybore's tongue had been cast away, hurled down the Road and hidden for all time. As a god he had that power. And as a god, he had the power to conjure himself a new tongue. She leaned her head on his shoulder.

He held his hand in front of his face and conjured a small spell. Some residual ability remained. Sharp, well-defined flames lanced from his fingertips. Since giving away the powers locked within him, though, Lan had concentrated on healing spells. He didn't doubt he was vastly better than either of the chirurgeons back in the town.

"The cenotaph will open in another hour," Inyx said. "Have you looked around enough?"

"More than enough," Lan assured her. He craned his neck and asked, "Where is he? I told him this cenotaph opened at sunset, not at midnight."

"He'll be here. He's probably out chasing after bugs."

Lan looked down into Inyx's blue eyes. "Do you have any regrets? About Ducasien?"

"None," she said. "Well, perhaps a little. He is a good man."

"He will rule well with Nowless and Julinne," said Lan.

"There'll be friction. Ducasien had his eye on Julinne. I don't think Nowless likes it."

"We can look in on them," promised Lan. "In a year or two."

He sighed as he thought of Brinke. So regal, so lovely. Her world destroyed, she had also become a traveler along the Road. One day their paths would cross. Lan knew it. He wished her only the best in her sojourn along the Road.

"Dammit," he yelled, "where are you, Krek?"

A dark lump rose up nearby and shook itself. Long, coppery-furred legs gleamed in the setting sun.

"I rested, friend Lan Martak, nothing more. The journey has been arduous. And you insist on bringing me to worlds where there is nothing edible. Look at those grubs. Tiny!"

"Well, go back to your own web and your Klawn and all the rest," Lan said in disgust. Krek sometimes got on his nerves.

"That will be unnecessary, at least for the time being," said Krek. "It was so generous of you to offer Klawn one of Claybore's arms. As the hatchlings eat it, the flesh regenerates. There will never again be starvation in my web. But I do so worry about how tainted their tastes might become."

Inyx shuddered at the mention. Too much of Krek's ferocity had rubbed off on Lan. He had placed the eternal arm where Claybore would feel the nip of mandibles for as long as there were hatchlings to feed. The dismembered sorcerer had forever to regret all he had done. With each piece of flesh painfully snipped off, devoured and then magically renewed, he would regret it.

Lan never said where he placed the other parts. Inyx feared they were even more diabolically hidden.

"Get into the cenotaph," Lan said. "The gateway's opening."

Krek lumbered forward and dropped down. He vanished almost instantly. Lan and Inyx looked at one another, smiled as they locked arms, and slipped off the edge and into the grave.

Together, they walked the Cenotaph Road again.

BESTSELLING
Science Fiction
and
Fantasy

☐ 47809-3	**THE LEFT HAND OF DARKNESS,** Ursula K. LeGuin	$2.95
☐ 16021-2	**DORSAI!,** Gordon R. Dickson	$2.95
☐ 80582-5	**THIEVES' WORLD™,** Robert Lynn Asprin, editor	$2.95
☐ 11456-3	**CONAN #1,** Robert E.Howard, L. Sprague de Camp, Lin Carter	$2.75
☐ 49142-1	**LORD DARCY INVESTIGATES,** Randall Garrett	$2.75
☐ 21889-X	**EXPANDED UNIVERSE,** Robert A. Heinlein	$3.95
☐ 87329-4	**THE WARLOCK UNLOCKED,** Christopher Stasheff	$2.95
☐ 05480-3	**BERSERKER,** Fred Saberhagen	$2.75
☐ 10253-0	**CHANGELING,** Roger Zelazny	$2.95
☐ 51552-5	**THE MAGIC GOES AWAY,** Larry Niven	$2.75

Prices may be slightly higher in Canada.

MORE SCIENCE FICTION ADVENTURE!